William H. McCartney, J. H Selwyn

The Bayonet

A Drama

William H. McCartney, J. H Selwyn

The Bayonet
A Drama

ISBN/EAN: 9783337343248

Printed in Europe, USA, Canada, Australia, Japan

Cover: Foto ©Andreas Hilbeck / pixelio.de

More available books at **www.hansebooks.com**

𝔄 𝔇rama, in 𝔉our 𝔄cts.

By WM. H. McCARTNEY (Major Muldoon), AND J. H. SELWYN.

.

NEW YORK.
1871.

DRAMATIS PERSONÆ.

Captain John Fitzhugh.
Lieut. Richard Connery.
" James Morgan.
" Henry Thompson.
Col. McManus.
Surgeon Walker.
Clarence King.
Hon. Arthur Moore.

Hon. Samuel Blowhard.
Col. Roland.
Miss Bessie Moore (subsequently Private Milroy).
Miss Eleanor King.
Mrs. John Fitzhugh.
Miss Clara Connery.
Mrs. Morgan.

SERVANTS.

William, servant to Capt. Fitzhugh.
Uncle Peter, cook to Capt. Fitzhugh.
Peter, Mr. Moore's servant.

Confederate Officer.
Federal Non-Commissioned Officers.
Soldiers, Citizens, Farmers, &c.

TIME.

1st Act, April, 1861.
2d Act, three weeks later.

3d Act, same time as last.
4th Act, 1863.

ACT FIRST.

SCENE FIRST.

(*Lawyer's office, of the firm Fitzhugh & Connery.*)

(*Connery is seen sitting face to the audience looking over a legal document, and office boy sits on a high stool.*)

(*As the curtain rises, — Enter Jas. Morgan, a law student.*) (*L.*)

Morgan. Good morning, Mr. Connery. Rather lively news this morning. Of course you know the President has called for troops to quell the insurrection? Indeed, sir, war seems inevitable, and the worst of all wars, — civil war. I wish —

Connery. (*Looks up for the first time, and interrupting M.*) Yes. Shouldn't wonder.

Morgan. Will you allow me to light a cigar, sir? and perhaps you will smoke? Pantelas; hardly up to the times, — mild, — but consoling. (*Proffers Connery a cigar.*)

Connery. Yes. Thank you. Then it is war, you think, Mr. Morgan? It occurs to me, that the people ought to be satisfied with such legal scrimmages as we are able to get up for them, — (*lights the cigar*) — where their losses are confined mostly to the pocket. But war, I take it, is a sort of national litigation, Mr. Morgan; and the book men tell us we must have it just about once in twenty years, — just as we have the violent cholera seasons, and just as, in other countries, they have the plague and other contagious diseases, — although I don't see any particular necessity for this war. But I suppose the politicians have arranged all that. Mr. Morgan, have we anything for trial to-day?

Morgan. (*Reading from a docket.*) Yes, sir. "State vs. Harding." The Harding case is down for to-day. Is it for trial?

1*

Connery. Harding — Burglar — That's one of Mr. Fitzhugh's cases, Mr. Morgan.

Morgan. Yes, sir.

Connery. Yes. I thought so. Fitzhugh tries his cases. That's a weakness of his, Mr. Morgan. Never try a criminal case, especially when the defendant is out on bail, as is this Harding, if you can get it postponed. Witnesses for the government die, — the district attorney forgets, that gentle sweet dame Justice grows blind with the lapse of time, and if we could only manage to have the policemen grow forgetful as they ripen in years — it would doubtless prove very gratifying to such men as Harding, and to a large but not very respectable class of our fellow-citizens.

(*Outside drums, cheers and shouting. M. moves to the window. C. remains seated.*)

Morgan. Troops, Mr. Connery. They seem to be recruits in all sorts of uniforms. Yes, and our man Harding is in the ranks. And they have, some of them, the number of Mr. Fitzhugh's regiment.

Connery. Yes. Soldiers, and the flag business. Mr. Fitzhugh's regiment paraded yesterday for inspection, I think. I apprehend that's what keeps him from the office so late this morning. Is it a part of Mr. Fitzhugh's regiment?

Morgan. (*Resuming his seat.*) They certainly had his regimental number.

Connery. That looks quite squally for the senior member of this firm. But Mr. Fitzhugh has always looked the soldier ; that is to say, so far as we Americans, who really know but little of that trade, can judge, and possibly, the time for action is near at hand. But I think we must report him missing from his engagement of yesterday.

(*Enter Fitzhugh.*) (*L.*)

Fitzhugh. Not if this judicial tribunal knows herself, and, gentlemen, she leans that way. But you will please allow me to suggest, that you two seem to be in league with the farmers, to raise the price of cabbages by burning them. Mr. Connery, I don't pretend to know enough

about. farming to warrant me in writing a book on that
subject, but I am willing to gamble that you bought that
cigar in Chatham street. Whew! James! (*To office
boy.*) James! please raise that window. (*He raises it
and resumes his seat.*) Gentlemen, those cigars are strong
enough and vile enough to stop a watch.

Morgan. (*Protesting.*) But, Mr. Fitzhugh. Excuse
me, I paid —

Fitzhugh. Oh! These were your cigars, were they?
(*Seats himself at his desk.*)

Mr. Morgan, if you really insist on smoking, please
take my advice and don't use that kind of vegetable?
That loquacious Chinaman who sells cigars opposite the
Astor House has a better brand than the Chatham-street
cabbage brand. Elevate your taste Mr. Morgan; elevate
your taste, and patronize the Pagan!
(*Looks over his papers.*)

Morgan. But, Mr. Fitzhugh, —

Fitzhugh. Certainly. But, as our Celtic friends say,
" *We will lave that go.*" How stands the docket to-day?
Have we any strong candidates for that blissful seat of
unwilling industry, Sing-Sing?

Morgan. Harding's case is down for to-day, sir. But
he don't seem to mind it much. I saw him out with a
squad of soldiers a short time since.

Fitzhugh. Mr. Morgan! You don't mean to tell me
that you saw that twice-convicted burglar with a uniform
on his back?

Connery. (*Interrupting.*) Yes. But he saw him
with part of a uniform on his back. And I must say, I
fail to see how it deprives a man of his right to become a
target to be shot at, to have been only twice convicted of
the comparatively mild offence of burglary. Besides, you
know, Mr. Fitzhugh, you ought not to complain, for you
defended him, and it was through your brilliant legal
strategy that he succeeded in getting into the State
prison.

Fitzhugh. (*Imitating C.*) Yes.

Connery. Yes. And while we are on the soldier question, (*he smokes*) please allow me to suggest for your
edification captain; that if there are people South so

rash and indiscreet as to have fired on the flag already, and the president has called on your militia duffers to gun those disturbers of the public peace in return, I am inclined to the belief, I say, that between you, you will manage to get up a first-class row, and if I mistake not, you will need the services of the entire Harding family before you get through.

Morgan. And, Mr. Fitzhugh, arn't you aware that there is something going on in the military line this morning?

Fitzhugh. Yes, gentlemen, as you both know our regiment was ordered to be in readiness some little time since, and when we received the order for the parade yesterday, I thought we were to be ordered away at once, although it hardly seems possible that the two sections of this country are really about to shoot each other like barbarians and maniacs, I can hardly work myself up to that belief. However, if it comes to a case of protecting the flag of the United States of America, you can just enter John Fitzhugh's name as appearing for the defence.

(*Drums outside again.   Morgan to the window.   F. and C. remain seated, still at their documents.*)

Morgan. Here comes that squad again.

(*F. to the window.*)

Fitzhugh. If that is not my orderly sergeant, I'm no militia man.

Morgan. They are coming this way, sir.

Fitzhugh. (*To Morgan.*) It looks like it, certainly. (*To Connery.*) Mr. Connery, the American Eagle begins to scream!

Connery. (*Without looking up.*) Yes; let him scream!

(*Rap outside.*)

Fitzhugh. Come in.

(*Enter Thompson, orderly sergeant of infantry.   (L.)   He salutes, places a paper on the desk, and resumes a stiff, soldierly appearance.*)

Sergt. Captain Fitzhugh.

(*F. takes the paper, runs his eyes over it, and starts. Cheers and drums outside.*)

Fitzhugh. Sergeant, will you please order those blood-thirsty patriots outside to repress their military ardor for a few moments? Just say to them, sergeant, that the chances are, they are likely to have plenty of the best of exercise for their lungs and legs shortly, in another quarter.

(*Sergt. salutes, retires* (*L.*), *noise ceases.*)

(*Reads.*) " Report with your command at 12." (*Looks at his watch.*) It is now half-past eleven. Regiment ordered away. Mr. Connery, didn't I tell you the national bird had commenced to flutter! Gentlemen, I am a peaceable man, you know, both of you, and if your evidence could be relied on, I think I could prove that fact before any tribunal in this State. And I am free to admit, that when I became a militia man, I had not the slightest idea that our people were ever going to shoot each other with the coarse shot of actual war. But my regiment is going, and I am going. For John Fitzhugh is not of that stuff which makes soldiers in peace and citizens in war. Mr. Connery, buy yourself a woolen shirt and a shot-gun. Snipe shot won't do for this kind of game. Mr. Morgan, ask the courts to continue my cases, or send them to Virginia for trial. I propose to sacrifice my clients on the altar of Mars. This (the order) admits me to practice before the highest tribunal in the land. The firm of Fitzhugh & Connery is dissolved. John Fitzhugh, Yankee, and Captain of the militia, appears for the American Union!

(*Enter Sergeant Thompson* (*L*), *salutes.*)

Segt. T. Any orders, sir?

Fitzhugh. Assemble the company, Sergeant. I will be at the armory at once. Dismissed.

(*The Sergeant salutes and turns.*)

Sergeant.

(*The Sergeant faces about.*)

Sergt. T. Sir?

Fitzhugh. Have you many recruits?

Sergt. T. All we need, sir. Find more than we can accept.

Fitzhugh.   Have you a recruit by the name of Harding?
Sergt. T.   Yes, sir; a strong, likely man.
Fitzhugh.   Yes, Sergeant; I always thought that man Harding would make a good soldier; and as the State seems likely to claim his services, if the Nation don't secure them at once we will accept him.
      Dismissed.

(*The Sergeant salutes, retires L.*)

(*Drums and shouting outside.   Morgan looks from the window as the squad retires to the rear of the stage.   Fitzhugh hastily arranged his papers to be sent to his house.   Connery sits quietly all the while without raising his eyes from his document.   Newspaper boy outside.*)

Boy.   (*Outside.*)   'Ere's the 'Erald, World and Tribune Extra!   News from the seat of war!   Two thousand men killed!

(*Morgan to the window.*)

Fitzhugh.   What's that?
Morgan.   A newsboy with some kind of war news.
Fitzhugh.   Call him in, Mr. Morgan.
Morgan.   (*Head out of the widow.*)   Here, boy, come in here. (*Enter boy.   L.*)
Boy.   'Ere's the 'Erald, World and Tribune Extra!   News from the seat of war!   Two thousand men killed!
Fitzhugh.   Hold up there, you newspaper agent!   Aren't you cutting that rather fat?
Boy.   (*To F.*)   Paper, sir?

(*Connery looks up.*)

Connery.   (*To boy.*)   Yes; if you go on at that rate, you will do away with any necessity for another census.
Boy.   (*To C.*)   Paper, sir?

(*All buy papers.*)

(*Boy retires crying his papers.*)

Boy.   'Ere's the 'Erald, World and Tribune Extra!   News from the seat of war!   Two thousand men killed!

(*Exit.   L*).

Fitzhugh. Bad news, this, Mr. Connery. Those Southern Comanches have commenced the war-dance. Won't you take a hand? Depends on the draw entirely. It may be a major-general's commission, and it may be a pine coffin-box.

Connery. Yes. Haven't a cigar with you, have you Captain?

Fitzhugh. Yes, I have; (*profferring it*) but do you mean to come out of your shell and support the flag? (*Connery lights the cigar.*)

Connery. Yes. I think perhaps we had better give up practice. I don't precisely see the necessity for all this. James, (*to office boy*) James. bring my coat. (*Puts it on.*) Thank you. James, take that box of papers to my house. Captain, I think I will buy that shirt. Mr. Morgan, the eagle is threatened with a military law suit. Shall we appear for the bird?

Morgan. With all my heart, sir; I go for the Union!

Connery. Yes; for the Union! Good morning, Captain, we will meet you at the armory. We are soldiers now, aren't we, Mr. Morgan? And in for the glory of getting shot, and having our illustrious names misspelt in the public prints. At the armory, Captain!

(*Exeunt. L.*)

Fitzhugh. Nor do I see the necessity for this bloodshed, and I shudder at the parting from my wife and child. A soldier has no business to be married, — but I was married before I became a militia man. Brace up, Captain! Brace up, John Fitzhugh! It is hard, I know. But the country calls for men, and who shall answer if we holiday soldiers decline? No! There is no halting here. For me, — for every loyal man — there is but one course to pursue, and it is pointed out in the doctrine of John A. Dix, and it is the highest law of the land: "If any man attempts to haul down the American flag, shoot him on the spot!"

(*Fitzhugh to the window to see the passing troops, as they now file past the rear of the stage from right to left. But not so as to be seen fairly by the audience. Their color only are seen, a small flag, and the tips of their bayonets They have two drums.*)

(*Scene closes. Flats in front.*)

ACT FIRST.

SCENE SECOND.

(A Public Square in a city.)

(Enter a squad of infantry troops from the left, preceded by two drums and a fife. They carry a small flag. Half way — across (towards the right); the Sergeant in command — Thompson.)

Sergt. T. Squad, halt! By the right flank, right face! In place, rest!

(They face the audience, Sergeant in front and right.)

Well, men, we are in for it. You have signed the rolls, and you are to all intents and purposes soldiers of the United States. But not legally so. until you have been mustered in by an officer representing the National Government. So that if there is any man here who is sick of his bargain, he has only to say so, and we will strike his name from the rolls, and fill his place with some other man. This, men, is the only chance you will have to express your choice in this matter. Consider it well, men!

Harding. Look here, Sergeant! We ain't none of us going to squeal, — we ain't, are we fellers?

All. No! No!

Sergt. T. All right, men. I am glad you are firm and true.

Harding. You bet!

Sergt. T. Now, men, this is your last chance. Who goes back on his country? *(Silence.) Sergt. grasps the colors; waves them.)* Who stands by the flag?

All. *(Tumultuously.)* We all do, — all of us.

(Harding steps to the front and faces the squad.)

Harding. Say, fellers! Three cheers for the flag! Now, wake 'em! *(Cheers.)* Three more for our Sergeant! Now, wake 'em again!

(Cheers, and he steps back into the ranks.)

Sergt. T. Thank you, men; I will try to deal square-ly by you all, and we will all of us do our whole duty, I trust, like men. After you are dismissed you will have an opportunity to visit your families; but you will report at the armory, every man of you, in just three hours; we are off to-night; we are in at the start; let us see this thing through. Attention Squad! (*They straighten up.*) Left face! Break ranks! March! (*All yell.*)

(Exeunt to R. and L.)

(Singing.)

Our Sergeant he's a first-class brick,
    Hurrah! Hurrah!
Our Sergeant he's a first-class brick,
    Hurrah! Hurrah!
Our Sergeant he's a first-class brick,
    And we'll follow his lead at quick double quick!
And we'll hop, skip, jump, boys,
    As we go marching on!
And we'll hop, skip, jump, boys,
    As we go marching on!

(Enter Harding. R.)

Harding. (*Meditating.*) Aren't this a rum go on the fly cops? Didn't I see that bloody fly cop, Smithers, fix his peepers on me, when I hove my name on that paper of the Sergeant's, and slid into these here trowsers (*looks at his trowsers*), and walked off on my left ear? Oh, no! I guess not! Why, here is Bill Harding gets to be some shakes when they want the raw material to make up into patriots, he does. Here was the State a putting in a claim to-day for my services in the stone hammering busi-ness. And I goes to Uncle Samuel, and I says, — Look here Guvnor, I'm good enough to be shot at — I am — and old Sam's man says, — Good boy, Bill! And I'm a soger, — I am, I don't mind no fly cops now, — I don't. (*Voice on the left singing,*

"And we'll hop, skip, jump, boys,
    As we go marching on.")

(Repeats.)

If that isn't Micky Scot, I'm a squealer — I am. (*Enter Scot. L.*)

Scot. Hullo, Bill!

Harding. Hullo, Scotty!

2

Scot. Say, Bill! I thought I saw you with them soger cops, just now?

Harding. Why, in course you did, Scotty. I am on my dead reform, — I am. This was my trial day, you know, Scotty, and them bloody fly cops thought they were going to send me up because I wouldn't blow on Patsy Reardon, — they did. But I've jined, — I have. I'm going to be a fighter, with a gun — I am — and our Sergeant, Scotty. Why, Scotty, you ought to see our Sergeant! He's a talker, — he is — one of them gentleman-fighters, Scotty. Won't I stay with that Sergeant? Rather! And he says to us fellers — You go home and see your old woman, and meet me at the station house in three hours. Oh, I'll be there, Scotty, — the fly cops be blowed! They be blowed!

Scot. You don't mean to say you are square on this, Bill? Regular reform, Bill, — no put up job?

Harding. In course it is. I ain't got no brace on 'em. That Sergeant gets me, — he does. You see, Scotty, I hain't done much yet in the moral citizen line, and I'm going on my good behavior, — I am. Say, Scotty — won't you jine? any quantity of new harness, Scotty. Look a-here, Scotty! (*Points to his trousers.*) Acres of grub, Scotty! And Scotty, you ought to see our Sergeant! We will come home patriot fellers, — we will, Scotty — or we will come home stiffs — toes up, Scotty. But on that lay it don't make no difference which. Does it, Scotty? Say, old pal, won't you jine?

(*Enter News Boy.*)

Boy. Here's the Erald, World and Tribune extra! News from the seat of war! Two thousand men killed!

Harding. See here, papers; you just leave here, or I will set on you, — I will.

(*Boy shies off.*)

Boy. Paper, sir? News from the seat of war! Two thousand men killed!

Scot. Say, Bill, — Them Southern chaps are worse nor the fly cops, — they are. Hear that, Bill? Two thousand men nailed in one day!

(*Boy discovers Harding's trowsers.*)

Boy. Why, set me up in a pea nut stand, if Bill Harding hain't nipped a pair of soger trowsers so quick!

Harding. See here, sonny; I don't want no more chin, — I don't — do you hear?

(*Strikes, — Boy avoids.*)

Boy. Paper, sir? News from the seat of war! Two thousand men killed!

Harding. Oh, blow your papers; I've jined, — I have. This (trowsers) ain't no prig, — this ain't.

Boy. Jined! Soger, won't you buy a paper?

Scot. Oh, come on, Bill; I'm game for this, — I am. But you may have me clubbed if I don't think a blue coat will make me sick. Say, Bill; can't we go in this kind of togs?

Harding. Come on, old pal; blue make you sick! Why, we are kind of military fly cops, — we are. Oh, blow the fly cops! They be blowed!

(*Exeunt R.*)

(*Boy stands watching them in astonishment.*)

Boy. Put me down for a sucker if this don't beat me! Bill Harding and Micky Scott going for sogers! Why, they can't do nothing but carry the target behind the fellers what has the guns,— they can't — and they might get a smoked Fenian to do that! Oh, bags! (*Moves to left.*) 'Ere's the 'Erald, World and Tribune Extra! News from the seat of war! Two thousand men killed! (*Exit. L.*)

(*Scene closes. Flats open.*)

ACT FIRST.

SCENE THIRD.

(*A Rail Road Station.*)

(*To be changed to suit locality.*)

(*Groups of people are standing and sitting about, of both sexes, and occasionally a soldier is seen.*)

(*Enter R.*)

MRS. JOHN FITZHUGH, wife of Captain Fitzhugh.

CLARA CONNERY, Lieut. Connery's sister.

MRS. MORGAN, Lieut. Morgan's mother, and —

CHILD, daughter of Mr. and Mrs. Fitzhugh.

Child. Why, mamma; I don't see the soldiers. Where is papa?

Mrs. F. The troops have not yet arrived, my child. Your father will be here presently, my dear.

Mrs. M. (*To Mrs. F.*) This is sad, indeed; I hear that your husband has secured commissions for Mr. Connery and my son James, and they are to accompany him as his officers. Although I can hardly realize that my darling boy is so soon to become a soldier, and battle with those hot-blooded, impetuous Southerners. But I suppose it's their duty.

Clara. Certainly, Mrs. Morgan. And not more beloved by you is your only son, the prop and support of your widowhood, than is my dear, old brother, Dick, by me. Oh, Dick! How much I love thee! But, madam, had I a thousand brothers, as much beloved even as is my manly, old Dick, I would give them ALL to the defence of my country! Aye, madam! I would shoulder a musket and go myself, but for these clumsy petticoats.

Mrs. F. Yes, Clara. I don't so much regret this on my own account, for I have long foreseen it; and I have called to my support what little philosophy I could muster to strengthen me in this hour of trial. But when I think of our child, Clara! And, Clara, if anything should happen to him! Think of it! The newspapers are already announcing fatal,— and I doubt not, to my families, the most heart-rending news — yet this is a man's duty, I suppose. And Captain Fitzhugh, though he is but a militia man, and is sometimes regarded as light and frivolous, is very determined, I assure you; as he is also, I am proud to say, very patriotic. Only, I do wish I had more of your courage, Clara. But we will not dishearten them with our tears. Oh, no! Let us send them away, if possible, with light hearts, and bid them godspeed, and a safe return.

Child. Oh, mamma! Here is a soldier with a gun so heavy, that it makes him lean over. (*Enter Timothy O'Callahan, private, quite drunk; and Mrs. O'C. L.*)

Mrs. O'C. Good avening, ladies! Is it here the sogers are coming, at all, at all? (*Private O'C. stands by badly mixed.*)

Mrs. F. Yes, my good woman! They start from this station. Have you any friends going into the service?

Mrs. O'C. Friends, did you say? Bad luck to the likes of me, but I have, though! Me ould man here, meself and Tim O'Callahan, have been friends, as much as married folks can be, these twenty years. And a bould, broth of a man he is too, — a rale sober, industrious man, and never gets drunk more nor four times a week,— Mum! But now he's gone and 'listed, mum. Bad luck to this sogering!

Mrs. F. (*To Tim.*) Do you know the name of your officer, sir? Perhaps we can assist you.

Tim. (*Taking off his cap and dropping his gun.*) Indade I do, mum. For he has a right to be an Irishman by the sounding of his name. Fitzhugh, mum, if you plaze, — Captain Fitzhugh, of the infantry.

Mrs. F. Yes, sir! We are also waiting for Captain Fitzhugh's company. Perhaps you had better take a seat there. I think he will be here presently.

Mrs. O'C. Thank you, mum! You're a perfect lady, mum! God bless you, mum! Oh! the likes of this!

2*

Bad luck to you, Tim O'Callahan, but I'll bate ye over the head wid a skillet when yez come home, if yez don't whale the blazes out of thim dirty blaguards, who are taking you from your quiet, paceful home.

Mrs. M. Oh, this wretched war! (*To Clara.*) Do you see that poor man just on the point of leaving his family, perhaps forever, and he is beastly drunk? It is not alone the risk of battle, I fear. But war is so demoralizing, and my boy is so young and impetuous. Then, there is the excitment of camp; and the recklessness of soldiers is proverbial, and —

Clara. (*Interrupting.*) My dear madam, please don't conjure up any evil forebodings. Aren't you sending away your son, who is not much of a chicken after all, in the same company with my brother Dick? And Dick, you know, as Mr. Ward says, "don't ever slop over." They are brother officers. And there is Capt. Fitzhugh, to give them life and good cheer; and the Captain knows something about war. Oh, how I wish I could see Dick in his uniform! Think of it, my dear madam, what a trio! The Captain, with his wit and good cheer,— your son, with his enthusiasm — and cool, solid old Dick, pulling away at his pipe! Soldiers always smoke pipes, you know, madam, — and breasting, like our northern granite, the traitorous tide of secession. I hear him now, in the midst of the din and smoke of battle, with shot and shell flying about him, and death at every hand — firm and unflinching, " *Steady there, men!*" and then he pulls away at his pipe again. Oh, how I wish I was a man!

(*Music outside, softly, in the distance; cheers and shouts.*

Clara at the window.)

Child. Oh, mamma! I hear the soldiers!

Mrs. F. Yes, my dear, it is quite time for them to come.

Child. Now I shall see my papa. He will have his sword, won't he, mamma? And he will bring the drums and the band. Isn't this jolly, mamma?

Mrs. F. (*With a sigh.*) Yes, my child. (*Aside.*) My darling husband goes forth to battle for his country,

the pride of his child,— his wife and his friends. I pray
to heaven he may safely return.

Clara. Yes, here they are! There is the Captain, Mrs.
Fitzhugh, as bright and cheerful as a true man ought to
be. Where is Dick? Oh, there is James, Mrs. Morgan;
where is Dick? Oh, I see him, now. He is p'odding
along with a book in his hand. Is not that like Dick?

(*Music nearer. Enter newsboy.*)

Boy. 'Ere's the 'Erald, World, and Tribune extra!
News from the seat of war! Three thousand men killed!
(*To Tim.*) Paper, sir? Three thousand men killed!

Mrs. O'C. Get out of this, ye spalpeen, wid your
three tousand killed! Just you wait till Tim O'Callahan
gets there! Bad 'cest to the thratorus blaguards!

Boy. Paper, mum?

Mrs. O'C. Och! but I'll bate yez to pieces!

(*Strikes at boy; he avoids. They move off to the rear.
Band enters the station.*)

Child. Oh, mother! See my papa!

Mrs. M. My poor son!

(*Troops file in.*)

Clara. Please don't show any grief, now, Mrs. Morgan, please don't! It will make them sad and gloomy.
Please don't!

(*Troops cross from right to left of stage, and take position
in line — band playing — officers in their proper places,
as the company reaches the proper position.*)

Capt. F. Company, halt! Front face! Order arms!
In place, rest!

(*Lieuts. C. & M. take positions in front with their lady
friends, Connery with Clara on right; Morgan with his
mother on the left; Mrs. Fitzhugh near the Captain.*)

Capt. F. I don't propose to make a speech, men; this
is no time for speeches; and besides, I don't propose to
make a George Francis Train of myself. I dont think
there is any of the Train blood in our family, which is not

celebrated for its speaking parts; and, as a rule, we appear best in protracted silence.

Connery. (*Aside.*) Yes!

Capt. F. Nor have I much of a Napoleonic campaign to lay before you. I don't think there is *much* Napoleonic blood in our family, not even of the Teutonic tinge of the present Napoleon. But I do wish to say, that I claim to have the theory of this case in my head, which amounts to just about this: that some one down South, — and it don't make any particular difference who — has fired on the flag, and we are called on to defend. I think I can look above party questions, — up to the Stars and Stripes — and I hope you are all blessed with the same patriotic powers of observation. And I wish to say further, that I think there is going to be the tallest kind of a row, and I propose to be enumerated therein. And when you break ranks, if there is a man among you, who has discovered since he enrolled himself, that he has important and private business relations which will require his personal attention here at home, we will forgive the judicious backslider, and fill his place with some other man. I think we can do that, can't we, Sergeant?

Sergt. T. Yes, sir; at once!

Capt. F. I thought so. Remember, men; backsliders will report to the 1st Sergeant in two minutes; and those who remain firm in the faith will report in just ten minutes, when we shall start for the bright and sunny South. Attention, company! Shoulder arms! By the right flank, right face! Remember, men; ten minutes with your families, and then for a few months.

How long did you say it would take us to march to the Gulf of Mexico, Mr. Connery?

Connery. Yes; how long, I didn't say. But I think it were better to calculate the time by years.

Capt. F. Oh, yes! *And then,* for a few months, be the same more or less, with Uncle Sam. Break ranks, march!

(*Soldiers scatter with shouts and cheers.*)

Child. Oh, papa! What a pretty sword!

Capt. F. (*His sabre is unslung, and in his hand.*)
Yes, my child. That is a very nice sword. Heretofore,
I have regarded that weapon as mostly ornamental; but
it seems now about to become useful; at least, that is the
theory of this business. Here, Orderly! (*Orderly comes
forward.*) Orderly, stow away this toad-sticker in some
safe place, I don't think I shall need it to-day. (*Orderly
takes the sabre.*) Mr. Connery, this young man will re-
lieve you of your Damascus, if it troubles you.

Connery. Yes. Thank you, Captain. But I think I
will keep it by me. It gives me confidence in myself.

(*Exit Orderly. R. Capt. Fitzhugh, wife and child retire
to the left and rear. Connery and Clara move to the
front.*)

Clara. Oh, Dick! I am so proud of you! Why,
you look as if you were born a soldier.

Connery Yes. But I feel, Clara, as if I had been
born a civilian of the most peaceful inclinations. I don't
quite like this costume. (*Pulls at his clothes.*)

Clara. And that book you were reading as you
came along. How discreet in you, Dick, to think of pro-
viding yourself with something to beguile your time.

Connery. Yes, Clara. This is a very cheerful and
beguiling book. (*Produces it.*) This is Hardee on Infantry Tactics. Sweet rhymes of the soldier's nursery.
Do you know, Clara, I had to consult this book to ascertain where I belong, in this patriotic arrangement of men?

Clara. (*She laughs.*) But you will know where to
be in a fight, Dick!

Connery. Yes; I think I shall know where I should
like to be, — I think *now* — I should prefer to be in the
major general's position, which is here described, as being at a comparatively safe distance in the rear.

Clara. (*She laughs.*) Oh, Dick! You are always
bantering, and always deceiving yourself. But I know
where you will be, and what you will do. You will be
where the fight is hottest, and glory is to be won.

Connery. Yes, glory! Thank you. (*Bugle blows the
assembly; Mrs. Morgan and James forward.*)

Morgan. Dear mother, soon we are off; I have arranged our business matters, I think, to your entire satisfaction and convenience. And, mother, I hope you will not yield to your gloomy forebodings.

Mrs. M. My darling boy! My only child, — God protect thee!

(*They move back — Tim and Mrs. O'Callahan forward.*)

Mrs. O'C. Here, Tim! (*T. staggers up, but is rather steadier than before.*) Don't yez hear the boogle?

Tim. That I do, Mrs. O'Callahan; I've heard that swate voice before, too, — bad cest to the thraitors!

(*Captain Fitzhugh now comes forward; Mrs. Fitzhugh and Mrs. Morgan together in the rear; Tim and Mrs. O'Callahan in front.*)

Mrs. O'C. (*To Capt.*) Captain Fitzhugh, if you plaze, sir! This is me old man, Tim O'Callahan, who goes wid yez to the wars, and he'll stay by yez, Captain, — that he will. But, plaze sir, sind me every cint of his pay. He's a sober, stout, broth of a man, sir, and kind to his family; but he has no skill in money matters, at all, at all. Here, Tim! Give a twist of yer arrum, and off wid yez, and give the thraitors the load of yez gun, the murthering whilps! (*He throws his arm about her neck and kisses her.*) Good bye, Tim!

Tim. Good-bye, Mrs. O'Callahan.

Mrs. O'C. Och, bad luck to this war! Whale the blazes out of thim, Tim, whale the blazes out of thim!

(*She moves to the rear.*)

Tim. That I will, Mrs. O'Callahan, as sure as I'm from County Cavin.

(*He moves to the company. Bugle blows again.*)

Capt. F. Sergeant Thompson!

Sergt. T. Here, sir.

Capt. F. Form the company outside, there, and have them get aboard, when the train will move in here, and we will get on.

(*Exit.*)

(*Sergt. T. outside; at the right and rear.*)

Sergt. T. Company, fall in!

(*They form outside, on the right.*)

Morgan. (*To his mother.*)   Mother, farewell!

Mrs. M.   Heaven save and protect thee, my son!

(*They embrace.*)

Connery.   Kiss me, Clara!   I believe in thee, and in my country.

Clara.   Dear, good Dick!

(*She bursts into tears which she tries to conceal. They remain together. Enter Sergeant Thompson. R.*)

Sergt. T. (*To Capt.*)   The company is formed, sir. Are you ready, sir?

Capt. F.   All present?

Sergt. T.   Yes, sir.

Capt F.   Ready, Sergeant.   Get them aboard.

(*Exit, Sergt. R.*)

(*Whistle blows*)   .

Sergt. T.   Break ranks, march!   All aboard!

(*Whistle again.*)

Capt. F.   My wife, — my child — farewell!   I shall return in safety; I feel certain of it.

(*Train moves out from the right towards the left, and shows in front soldiers at the windows, crowding, yelling, cheering, &c-, and halts.*)

Mrs. F.   I am firm — God bless you!

Child.   Good-bye, papa!   Come home to morrow!

(*All shake hands — Mrs. F., Mrs. M., Clara and Child together. — Whistle blows. — Bell rings. — Capt. Fitzhugh, Lieuts. Connery and Morgan, move towards the train.*)

Capt. F.   All aboard, Sergeant?

Sergt. T.   All aboard, Captain.

Capt. F.   Steady there, men!   (*Silence.*)   Three cheers for the flag!

(*They cheer.*)

Sergt. T.   Three cheers for our officers!

(*They cheer. — Whistle blows. — Bell rings. — Train moves slowly.*)

Harding.   Three cheers for our Sergeant and ourselves!
Now wake 'em!

(*They cheer.*)

Capt. F.   (*To his officers.*)   Come, gentlemen.

(*Band,— or drum-corps, as it may be though' advisable, but
band would be better — now plays.   Ladies, — Mrs.
O'Callahan, Newsboy on his head, spectators, &c., are in
tableau.*)

(*Curtain down.*)

ACT SECOND.

SCENE FIRST.

CAMP IN THE FIELD.

(*On the right and rear there is an officer's wall tent.   On
the left and back still further Sibly tents (circular), for
the men, — about half-way between the two a field
piece, artillery, sentry on duty near the piece, with sabre.
Infantry sentry paces in front of all.   The men are
moving and lying about, or cooking, bringing wood or
water, or burnishing their pieces, or their field piece.
The costumes of the men are varied; some wear coats,
others do not.   But there is not a white shirt on the
stage, — all woollen of any color.   Capt. Fitzhugh and
Lieut. Connery are asleep on the straw in their tents.
Time — six A. M.   Sergt. Thompson leaves his quarters, moves to the officer's quarters — enters and shakes
Lieut. Connery.*)

Connery.   Yes.   What's up!

Sergt. T.   Drill in five minutes, sir.

Connery.   Yes.   Thank you.

(*Sergeant back to near his quarters; mingles with the men;
Connery arises, lights a pipe — boots and coat on, —
moves to the entrance of his quarters.   Looks out.*)

Connery. Yes. Rather more cheerful than our last camp. Three weeks in this country, and I believe we have seen pretty much all there is of this thing, excepting the shooting, which I am free to admit, I have no especial desire to see. But it is deuced mean business, though. The romance is gone, and the reality of marching, camping, picket and guard duty, and false alarms is a bore. (*Reaches back for a canteen and attempts to drink, but it is empty.*) Yes; the Captain's boy, William, has paid his respects to my canteen again. These colored people are too much given to the larceny of whiskey. (*Drums beat and bugle blows the drill-call together.*) Sergeant Thompson? (*Sergeant approaches.*)

Sergt. T. (*Salutes.*) Here, sir!

Connery. Form the company for drill, Sergeant, if you please.

Sergt. T. Yes, sir.

(*Salutes, moves to his quarters.*)

(*Connery into his quarters.*)

Sergt. T. Company, fall in for drill!

Sergt. B. Squad, fall in for drill.

(*Subordinate Sergeants about the camp repeat.*)

Sergts. Fall in for drill!

Sergts. Fall in for drill!

(*The Sergeant T. forms the company in the rear.*)

Sergt. T. Attention, company! Right dress! Front! Shoulder arms! By the right flank, right face!

(*Connery moves to the company, which remains under the command of the Sergt. T.*)

Forward, march!

(*They move off to the left and rear — the Artillery Sergeant forms on the piece.*)

Sergt. B. Attention, squad! Right dress! Front! Right face! To your posts, march!

3

(*The Sergeant of Artillery drills his men in the loading and firing of the piece as quietly as possible and slowly. Sergeant Thompson continues to exercise and drill the company, moving it from left to right,* IN THE REAR AND BACK. *Connery follows about, making a suggestion now and then, such as,* — "*Steady there! Keep your time! One, two; one, two. Draw in your chin, Scot!*" — *Singing is heard without.* — *William, the Captain's servant. This must not be a concert or minstrel nigger, but a plantation darkey, of a semi-religious comic turn of mind. He must wear military trousers, and he can wear a civilian's coat or a cavalry jacket, or any other kind of a uniform. But he must be clean, and not ragged.*)

William. (*outside.*)

> "De day ob Jubilee am coming,
> White folks, bress de Lord!
> De day ob Jubilee am coming,
> Brack folks, bress de Lord!"

(*Enters. Sneaks into the captain's quarters, singing softly, repeating.*)

> "Brack folks, bress de Lord! Brack folks, bress de Lord!"

(*Harding watches William.*)

Harding. (*Aside.*) If that moak goes through the Captain's canteen, this morning, we shall have a sick nigger in camp,— we shall.

(*William steals a long pull from the Captain's canteen, repeating, "Brack folks, etc." Takes the Captain's boots, and seats himself outside the tent, left and in front, and commences to brush them. Sings as he brushes.*)
William.

> Oh, ain't I glad I'se out ob de wilderness,—
> Out ob de wilderness;
> Oh, ain't I glad I'se out ob de wilderness!

Go away, dar. (*Brushes a fly.*) Brack folks, bress de Lord.

(*Harding watches. Left rear.*)

De day ob— (*Yawns.*) De day ob jubi — le — am (*Yawns.*)— de day ob ju — bi — lee — am com —(*Asleep over his boots.*)

Harding. Here, moak; wake up there!

(*William starts.*)

William. Sah?

Harding. Wake up, I say. Do ye hear?

William. Oh yes, sah! I'se awake, sah! Only fooling, sah!

(*Harding off.*)

William. (*Singing and brushing.*) De day ob ju—bi—lee.

(*Asleep again. Harding near.*)

Harding. Blow me, if that dose was enough for the moak.

(*William twists and writhes in agony.*)

What? Oh, yes; he's a sick nigger,— he is.

(*Retires to the rear and left.*)

William. Golly! Golly! massa Captain! What's de matter wid dis yere nigger? (*Gives a nigger yell.*) As true as Moses! Yere is a dead nigger! (*Yells.*) What am de matter wid dis yere child? Dat whiskey's alive! (*Harding, nearer.*) I'm a dead nigger for sartain! I'se dead, shuah? (*On the ground. Capt. F. awakes — upon his bed.*)

Capt. F. See here! You ebony prince of the House of Congo — what's the row here? (*Looks for his boots.*) William, where's my boots? (*Aside.*) What is the matter with that boy? (*To the entrance of his quarters — discovers William rolling on the ground.*) I believe the boy is sick, or is he fooling again? No! That is genuine distress. Here! Some one, — Orderly! Orderly! (*Harding appears.*)

Harding. Yes, sir! Here, sir!

Capt. F. Orderly, go for the doctor! (*Harding stands still.*) William must be sick — He don't seem to be fooling — Come, Orderly! I don't want a funeral in this camp, just now!

William. I'se a dead nigger! I'se a dead nigger!

Capt. F. Do you hear that, Orderly? Come! Why don't you start?

(*Harding hands the Captain his boots — He puts them on.*)

Harding. (*Aside.*) It is all right, Captain! All right, sir! This is my lay, — this is!

(*William groans.*)

Capt. F. Oh! This is your lay is it? Well, you seem to have laid him out pretty effectually; supposing you put him on his pegs again. What did you do to him Harding? You did'nt offer any violence to that poor bone of national contention, did you, Harding?

(*Last sharply.*)

William. I'se a dead nigger dis time, shuah!

Harding. Oh no, Captain, you don't think that; you don't believe I would abuse a poor nigger, oh no ; my game is bigger nor niggers ; I go for white game — I do ; I only dosed your canteen, cos I heard you say some one was prigging your commissary, and I wanted you to know it wasn't me. That's all. Ask him to histe, Captain, ask him to histe.

(*William groans*)

Capt. F. So, so! (*Aside.*) Oh you wretched Ethiopian! (*To H.*) Bring the canteen. (*Harding gets it.*) Here William, take a drop of this whiskey. I think you must have a touch of the colic. This climate don't seem to agree with you.

(*William groans.*)

William. Oh, massa captain! I nebber will touch dat canteen agen, nebber, nebber!

Capt. F. Oh, ho! Your usual morning cocktail don't seem to agree with you. (*William groans.*) Well, it's all right, only, in the future, you had better let me mix your drinks for you. Orderly, help up the boy and take him to his quarters, and let him sleep this off. And, Harding, no more of this ; I prefer to doctor my own family. And Harding, supposing I had happened to take an eye-opener before William came in! No more of this, I say!

Harding. I beg your parding, Captain, I didn't mean no harm, — I didn't.

(*Harding helps William up.*)

Capt. F. It's all right, Harding. (*To William.*) Feel kind of sea-sick, don't you, William? That whiskey is very strong. It was made for white soldiers, and it is entirely unsuited to the tender African stomach.

(*They, Wm. and Harding, move off to the rear and left.*)

William. I believe ye, I believe ye, massa Captain!

(*Capt. F. moves into his quarters, lights a pipe. While this has been going on, the artillery squad has been drilling.*)

Sergt. B. Squad to the front! March! Halt! Front face! By the right flank! Right face! Break ranks, march!

(*They disperse. Sergt. T. now marches the company back to the place where it formed.*)

Sergt. T. Company, halt! By the right flank, right face! Break ranks, march!

(*It disperses. Connery moves to his quarters.*)

Connery. Good morning, Captain.
Capt. F. Good morning, Mr. Connery. Has Mr. Morgan returned from the picket yet?
Connery. I think not, sir; hardly time yet.
Capt. F. That was a fearful march we had, getting here yesterday, Mr. Connery.

(*They lounge about on the straw.*)

Connery. Yes, rather.
Capt. F. .It all comes of these paper major-generals. Here is a man who was a tolerably successful criminal lawyer before he became a major-general, who reads in a book written by some other paper-fighter, that a man takes so many inches at a step, and that a healthy man can take so many steps in a day. Then he multiplies the number of inches the man usually takes by the number of steps he ought to take, and he figures up, — that raw troops from the North can march thirty-one miles in a day, in a burning, Southern sun. And he makes us do it, too. The theory may be good enough in peace times, on

3*

a drill ground; but the practice is rather uncomfortable in this locality,—eh, Mr. Connery?

(Both smoke.)

Connery. Yes; it's all of that.

Capt. F. Mr. Connery, How's your feet? Mine feel like boiled hams.

Connery. Yes; I think mine are slightly parboiled.

(Capt. F. moves to the entrance to his quarters.)

Capt. F. Have you been out round here, much, Mr. Connery? What kind of a neighborhood is this? Are the natives hospitable? Crops well started,—plenty of fence rails? Don't it strike you as rather remarkable, that the rude Northern soldier should prefer dry fence rails and window-shutters and house-blinds, to cutting good green oak? These children of the North are rather fastidious about their fuel. I overheard Harding telling that man, Scot, that he calculated he had burnt four hundred and fifty-nine dollars' worth of fence rails, at ten cents apiece, since we came into this country.

Connery. Yes; the Southern mind was "fired up" on patriotism, and our fellows seem to be "firing up" on fence rails,—which tends to keep both sides warm.

Capt. F. Oh, yes—I see. But it is one of the results of war, which is *commonly destructive* of fences and poultry. I see the General has favored us with strict orders against foraging. I hope you are doing all you can to assist me in impressing on the men the great importance of that order. The rights of property in this locality must be preserved.

Connery. Yes; I don't think the men disturb any property unless they want it.

Capt. F. That is correct, Mr. Connery,—that is soldierly, sir.

Connery. Yes; soldierly. But I don't know precisely what we have in the mess; chickens, perhaps; I saw Harding with half a dozen.

Capt. F. That man Harding is a very able commissary, Mr. Connery; but he comes honestly by those unfrequent trifles which go to make up our daily bread—don't he?

Connery. Yes; I don't doubt it.

Capt. F. I hope so; there can be no doubt about it, and I couldn't think for a moment of living on food illegally, or clandestinely obtained from our Southern brothers, oh no! It would not set well on my Federal stomach.

(*Captain Fitzhugh steps outside.*)

Mr. Connery, as this is our first morning here, I think I will look about a bit. This seems to be a fine country for agriculture. It occurs to me, those green slopes must support the gentle sheep and calf, so beloved by our rude barbarians and mud-sills. Orderly! (*Harding appears.*) Harding, you were on orderly duty, yesterday?

Harding. Yes, sir; my time is up at eight o'clock.

Capt. F. Well, do you know Harding, I think this country ought to be explored. Harding, look about over these green hills, you might find a sheep mine. And, Harding, if there is any kind of food in this wicked, rebellious country I prefer, it is lamb. I could put up with mutton, but I prefer lamb. You are excused from duty to-day, Harding; I will be here at breakfast, Mr. Connery.

(*Exit L.*)

Harding. Thank you, Captain.

Connery. Yes; the Captain is a faithful soldier, and a cheerful companion. But he is getting rather demoralized in his notions about food. But, then, you can't conduct a war as you would run a sabbath school! I think a nap until breakfast will do me no harm.

(*He reclines; scene closes; flats in front.*)

ACT SECOND.

SCENE SECOND.

(*A Southern grove (cultivated), near a gentleman's residence.
— Not tropical — oak, maple, cedar and hemlock trees
interspersed, with here and there a cluster of laurels. —
There is a rustic open seat in the middle of the stage.*)

(*Enter.*)

BESSIE MOORE, daughter of the Hon. Arthur Moore.
ELEANOR KING, her friend and companion.

(*They move to the seat.*)

Bessie. It is now three months, Eleanor, since your
brother Clarence, my Clarence, — the only beloved of
Bessie Moore — left us to enter the service of his country — the glorious, patriotic, and yet destined to be, the
free and independent South! Three months, Eleanor, and
it seems as if it were an age. But the letter! (*Looking
about.*) Where is the letter? Read it; please read it?

Eleanor. (*Looking about and feeling for the letter.*) I
hope it is not wicked, this clandestine correspondence.
What would your father say, if he should happen to hear
of it? Poor Bessie! And I am so happy,— indeed I am,
to be able to assist you in this matter. (*Produces the
wrong letter.*) Oh, that is from my lover!

Bessie. I don't wish that one.

Eleanor. No, of course not! But, Bessie, how could
you hear from him at all, but for me?

Bessie. Wicked! No Eleanor, it is not wicked to love
a man like Clarence, though he is poor. (*Eleanor starts.*)
Please excuse me, Eleanor; you know I meant no offence.

Eleanor. Oh, I don't take any offence from you, Bessie
Moore, on that account. For, in loving my brother, to
whom your father only objects because he is poor, you have
proved yourself nobler, in that respect, at least, than is
your father.

Bessie. Eleanor, remember! He is my father! But let us drop this subject. This clandestine correspondence troubles me a little, though. Wicked! It may not be quite right to be engaged to Clarence without my father's consent or knowledge, but there is no sin in letter-writing. And besides, I love him ; and love, they say, cuts curious capers. And, is it not necessary, sometimes, to sin a little to love very much?

Eleanor. I don't know, Bessie.

Bessie. But the letter ; read the letter, please.

Eleanor. Why, no. It is not for me to read. (*Feels for it.*) Where did I put that letter? Have I dropped it? You see, Bessie, I was terribly frustrated when your father entered the room just as I opened my letter, and found yours enclosed. Oh! Here it is! (*Hands it to B.*) And while you are reading it, Bessie, I will look about a step : for, next to being alone with one's lover is being alone with a letter from one's lover. (*Eleanor moves off. —L.*) (*Aside.*) Clarence, my dear brother, I wonder if you will ever marry Bessie Moore? (*Exit. L.*)

Bessie. (*Reads.*) " We have been here in camp two months." Dear, noble Clarence! His country first and always. And they are coming North. (*Looks up.*) Yes, and then : Woe to ye, ye burning, pillaging ruffians, who are despoiling our dear old State.

(*A bugle is heard in the distance faintly. Re-enter Eleanor.*)

Eleanor. Bessie! Bessie! There are troops near here. Did you not hear the trumpet?

Bessie (*without looking up*). Yes, Eleanor ; I know it. To our shame and sorrow, I know it

Eleanor. Then why did you not tell me?

Bessie. (*Still reading.*) I did not think it worth the while to waste my breath on those horrid Federal hirelings, who come down here to shoot and rob our Southern people. And, besides, they only came so near last night, papa says,— but please don't interrupt me, Eleanor.

Eleanor. No ; I don't wish to interrupt you, Bessie. (*Aside.*) It takes her so long to read that letter. But, Bessie, I did not know they were here. Where are they encamped?

Bessie. It is only a company. I heard papa say they only came here to establish an outpost, or something of the sort. The company is near the railroad yonder. The main body of troops is four or five miles away. But don't Eleanor, please don't. (*She reads.*) "And you continue firm and true, — I know you do, my love." Indeed, Clarence; indeed, do I.

(*Eleanor is impatient. — Bugle blows again*)

Eleanor. There it is again, Bessie. Do you hear it?

Bessie. Yes, Eleanor, I hear it! And I wish the instrument and the creature who blows it, were ten thousand miles away. (*Bessie takes out a locket, looks at it.*) True to thee, Clarence. (*Proudly.*) I am a Moore! (*Resumes letter.*)

Eleanor. Why! Bessie, have you not finished that letter yet? (*Aside.*) But this is her first, and Bessie is very affectionate. (*Bessie folds and puts away the letter.*)

Bessie. Yes, Eleanor, I have finished it; and I thank you for your kindness in suggesting to Clarence to send it to you, as otherwise I could not well hear from him; and I am rejoiced and happy to know that he is true to his country, and to me.

Eleanor. But I don't quite like the idea of his becoming a soldier, Bessie. Soldiers are awful creatures, aren't they? I remember to have heard some one say, that a man drops all the finer instincts of his nature when he takes up the sword.

Bessie. Oh, no! Eleanor. A gentleman is true to himself in camp, or in the drawing-room. Think of your brother; could he be anything but a gentlemen, in peace or in war?

Eleanor. Clarence? I know; but he is unlike most men. Bessie, I wonder what these Federals are like?

Bessie. I don't know, and I don't wish to know. I hear the North is sending the scum and filth of all its large cities into our beautiful Southern country; be that as it may. I don't wish to set my eyes on one of them.

Eleanor. But, Bessie, I do. I wish to know what kind of people my brother will have to fight. I hear they are mostly foreigners. If this company is near the railroad, we can see it from the brow of the hill there. Bessie, let's go and see them.

(*Takes her hand.*)

Bessie. No, no.

Eleanor. Please do? I don't think they are badly disposed towards us; you know the general sent us over a guard for the house, several days since. Come; they will do us no harm.

Bessie. Harm! Harm us! I fear no harm from them. I should like to see one of the ruffians come near enough, Bessie Moore, to offer any harm! The miserable wretches!

Eleanor. Oh, never mind that! You know I hate them as much as any one; but I wish to see them. Come, Bessie, it is only a step. Please come.

(*Exeunt. L. Enter two soldiers. They peer about.*)

1st Sol. Say, Jack, have we lost them? They came this way — two of 'em. The stunninest gals I ever seen, Jack! (*Looks about.*) I wonder which way they went?

2d Sol. Yes, Jim, — I know. But this is in that Fitz — something's limits, — this is — and he was a lootenant that's down on this thing, — he was. They are a hard pair for what they calls discipline, — they are. Suppose they should see us, Jim! Oh! let's drop this!"

1st Sol. They! Why, what have they to do with us? We aint under their command, — we aint. This is a free country, — this is. Aint we got as much right here as them high-backed officers? I guess we have!

2d Sol. Oh! I'm game for a lark! But, suppose the girls should be real ladies, Jim? They will make it warm for us. I couldn't face a real lady, no how, — I couldn't.

1st Sol. You are squealing, are you? Oh, come on!

(*Exeunt. L.*)

(*Screams without.*)

Bessie. Help! help! Father! James!

(*All rush on. L.*)

Eleanor. Help! help! What in Heaven's name do you mean, men? Help! help!

1st Sol. Now, see here, old gal, I don't want no noise
— I don't.

2d. Sol. Say, Jim ; let's drop this game.

(*Bessie stands firm.*)

Bessie. What do you mean, you miserable wretches?
Do you know you are on a gentleman's grounds who
would shoot you, as he would any other kind of vermin,
were he here? Do you come South to offer violence to
ladies? You are model Federal soldiers! Begone, you
dogs!

(*Eleanor crouches near Bessie.*)

Eleanor. Bessie, don't excite them. Please don't,
Bessie.

1st Sol. Shoot me, eh? Me a dog? The devil he will!

(*The soldiers rush at the ladies — 1st soldier at Bessie, 2d
soldier at Eleanor. Stage business. Enter Capt. Fitzhugh from the rear and right.*)

Capt. F. I thought I heard a woman scream. (*Discovers the soldiers and ladies struggling. Draws his sabre
quickly, by extending his arm at full length. To soldiers.*)
Here, you ruffians; take your hands off those ladies!
(*Soldiers do not see and do not heed him.*) Don't understand my English? I wonder how this will affect you.
(*Knocks down 1st soldier with the flat of his sabre. 2d
soldier, turning, discovers his comrade down, and the Captain evidently meaning business. He releases Eleanor, who
darts off. R.*)

2d Sol. Say! You Captain! Did you strike my pal?

(*Captain Fitzhugh makes at him.*)

Capt. F. Yes; you whelp! And if you don't lie flat
on your face until my guard comes, I will slice you into
sandwich meat. Turn out the guard! Turn out the
guard!

2d Sol. Oh, you will, will you! (*Draws and presents a pistol.*) See here, my fine duck! I ain't none of
your gang, and I ain't on duty ; and if you move out of
your tracks, until me and my pal gets away from here,
I will let daylight into you, — I will!

(*Enter Harding — Rear and left. — He hears the soldier's last speech. — Discovers pistol, and knocks the soldier down, — striking from behind.*)

Harding. Shoot my Captain, will yer! Oh, no! I guess not! (*Jumps on him. — The first soldier begins to revive. — Harding jumps on him.*) And you, too! You are in this gang, are you?

(*Second soldier begins to arise, when William rushes on him from the right, and butts him down.*)

William. What was yer doing to de Captain? (*Butts.*)
Capt. F. (*Bessie shows faintness.*) Harding, the lady faints! Water — quick — water!

(*Bessie faints in Capt. Fitzhugh's arms. — Harding rushes off to the left for water. — William points pistol at soldiers. Tableau. — if there is a second tableau, Eleanor can come on, with help.*)

(*Curtain down.*)

ACT THIRD.

SCENE FIRST.

(*Residence of a wealthy Southerner. But it is not a planter's residence, for it indicates more cultivation and refinement than is usually seen about a planter's home. Residence on the* RIGHT, — *on the* LEFT *there is a sort of rustic seat under a vine and trellis-work, which two persons could use for private conversation, without being overheard by the servants about the house. Hon. Arthur Moore, the proprietor, is seated on the portico, which is extensive. It is in early June, and the shrubbery is in full foliage and luxuriant. Time, three weeks after last Act, between 10 and 11 A. M. As the curtain rises, two ladies, Bessie Moore and Eleanor King, in morning costumes, step out of the house on to the portico.*)

Mr. Moore.   Well, ladies; are you going out for a walk? Fine morning this, ladies.

Bessie.   Yes, papa; we have had no exercise these several days!

Eleanor.   Yes, Mr. Moore; Bessie has suddenly discovered the necessity for exercise, — and she seems to prefer it in the company of the Captain, — although she concludes to take me this morning.

(*Eleanor laughs.*)

Bessie.   Eleanor! Why will you talk so? Is not the Captain a Northerner, and — and —

Eleanor.   And what, Bessie?

Bessie.   Oh! Fie on you, Eleanor! (*Aside to Eleanor.*) A married man, you dunce! (*And to Mr. Moore.*) A polite, gentlemanly officer, if he is a Northerner. Is he not, papa? And ought we not to be grateful to him, all of us?

Mr. M. Indeed, he is ! The Captain has been a heap of benefit to me, ladies. (*Aside.*) But I will turn our acquaintance to good account And, ladies, I hope you will show him all the attention your position and sex will permit.

Eleanor. Oh, yes, sir ! We will ! Indeed, we will ! Won't we, Bessie?

Bessie. Eleanor, I am ashamed of you ! Good morning, papa.

Eleanor. Good morning, sir.

Mr. M. Good morning, ladies. (*Exeunt. L, Mr. Moore leaves the portico for the rustic seat.*) Why not? He is a married man to be sure; I have ascertained that fact, through my lawyers. But he is not wealthy; only a lawyer and a captain. I can give him wealth and rank; such, indeed, as he probably never dreamt of. He can't possibly think of getting much promotion where he now is ; our people will make quick work of these fellows, as fast as they can be sent here. I think he agrees with me on that subject; and I am resolved to test him. (*Looks at his watch.*) It's now half past ten. I asked him to be here at eleven. (*Takes a parchment commission from his pocket.*) And I have secured him this commission. (*Reads.*) " John Fitzhugh of the Confederate States of America." (*Chuckles.*) Yes ! He will be of the Confederate States, *when he accepts !* " Brigadier General " ! (*Reads another paper.*) " General Fitzhugh will report for staff duty at the Adjutant's office, at Richmond." Indeed ! That would secure a less ambitious man than is the Captain, if I mistake not. If I can only manage to keep him from disclosing this to that Lieut. Connery, — I don't like that fellow. I can make nothing, whatever, of that cool, calculating lawyer,— who is as thoroughly disciplined as a faro bank dealer, with his mild, eternal " *yes,*" and even temper. He is the first man I ever saw impervious to wine and flattery.

(Enter Col Roland.)

Col. Mr. Moore, good morning, sir !

Mr. M. Colonel, I'm glad to see you, sir, — indeed, I am, sir ! Take a seat, sir. I hope your family is well, sir. Beautiful day, sir.

(*Colonel bows continually.*)

Col. Thank you, sir.

Mr. M. Peter! Peter! Ho, Peter!

Peter. Yere I is, sah.

Mr. M. Go into the library, Peter, and bring me that bottle of whiskey. (*Peter is kicking the ground.*) Do you hear, Peter?

Peter. Yes, sah.

Mr. M. And two glasses, Peter.

Peter. Yes, sah.

(*Peter moving to the house.*)

Mr. M. I'm right glad you've come, Colonel, — indeed I am. I sent the Captain a note with his breakfast, this morning, asking him to be here at eleven, and he says he will be here, sir.

Col. That's a right clever dodge, sir,— furnishing the Captain with his breakfast every morning, sir. John Randolph, or some other Southerner, said in Congress some years ago, sir, " If you want to hit a Yankee, strike him in the pocket, sir." But I reckon I can improve on that, sir. If you want to win the good will of a Yankee Captain, give him his breakfast, sir. A breakfast starts a man for the day, sir. A good breakfast makes him a gentleman, sir. But a bad breakfast makes him as surly as a bear, — as surly as a bear, sir! You can't manage a man on an empty stomach, or on one badly filled. Eh, sir? Indeed you can't, sir.

(*Re-enter Peter with glasses, etc. — They fill, touch, and drink together.*)

Mr. M. to Col. Our cause, — the South.

(*They drink. Exit Peter, with glasses, etc., into the house.*)

Col. And you think he will accept, sir?

Mr. M. He can't help it, sir. He is spooney on my daughter, sir. And she takes to him right smart, sir. At least, there is more than the ordinary amount of regard between them, sir. And then, the rank and the wealth, — wealth, sir.

Col. Yes, sir. That first meeting of theirs was calculated to inspire something of that sentiment, sir ; but
still, that part of the case gets me, sir. How will you
manage it, sir?

Mr. M. Why, Colonel? If he accepts the commission, he accepts the whole case, sir. There is no half-way
here, sir. I shall send Bessie south in his charge. I
have already deeded to her the Alabama estates in his
trust — I think they can manage the rest, sir,— yes, sir.

Col. But, my dear sir, have you broached the subject to Bessie? Does she know of it, sir?

Mr. M. Indeed, I have not, sir! That would never
do while she is under Mrs. Moore's eyes; no, sir! An
obstinate woman, my wife, sir. She won't even consent
to show herself when the Captain is about, sir. Although
I think she admires the Captain ; but she has too much
grit, sir. Too much Southern grit to show it, sir. Yes,
sir!

Col. And have you spoken to him of the attack to-
night, sir?

Mr. M. Colonel, I have not, sir. I only received your
letter announcing your purpose, this morning, sir. Perhaps we had better postpone it until we get his answer, sir.

Col. Impossible, sir! Impossible! Our people are impatient to get at these folks here, who are really isolated
from the main body of their troops ; and I have had all I
could do to restrain them so far, — yes, sir ; all I could
do, sir. The Captain in charge of the party is at my house
now, sir! Yes, sir! There now, sir!

Mr. M. There now, Colonel, is not that rather
reckless and indiscreet, sir? Suppose some of your niggers inform on us, sir?

Col. Oh, never mind that. Leave my niggers to me,
sir. I know them, sir.

Mr. M. But, Colonel, I insist on this : whether the
Captain accepts or declines, he must not be harmed to-
night, sir! No, sir, — not harmed, sir!

Col. I think that can be arranged, sir! Yes, sir!
(*Aside.*) He and his Lieutenant are just the game we are
after. But we attack his post to-night — sure, sir! Indeed, we will, sir!

3*

Mr. M. (*Looks at his watch.*) It is time for him,—
he is. very punctual, Colonel — will you please walk into
the library, sir; let me sound him alone, sir, if you please,
sir. (*Col. re-enters the house.*) I don't like this business of
to-night! What if he declines my proposals? And shall I
post him as to the attack? That would not do. (*Moves to
portico. — Looks up.*) Oh! Here he is! (*Enter Capt.
F. — He moves to the portico.*) I am glad to see you,
Captain.

Capt. F. Thank you, Mr. Moore.

Mr. M. Indeed I am, sir! Take a seat, sir! (*Proffers
chair on portico.*)

Capt. F. Thank you.

(*They sit or not, as may seem desirable.*)

Mr. M. How do you feel, sir? Fine weather, sir! A
wonderful climate we have here, sir!

Capt. F. Yes; Mr. Moore. This is a very pleasant
climate. (*Aside.*) Oh, Oh! Whither blows the gentle
Southern zephyr?

Mr. M. The ladies are out for a short walk, sir! They
will be here presently, sir — yes, sir! Here! Peter! —
Ho, Peter!

(*Re-enter Peter from the house.*)

Peter. Yere I is, sah!

Mr. M. Peter, go into the library and bring me that
bottle of whiskey. (*Aside to P.*) Find Miss Bessie.

Capt. F. If you please, Mr. Moore, — if you sent for
the bottle on my account, I prefer not to take anything this
morning — I don't feel just right.

Mr. M. It will do you good, — do you good, sir. A
soldier, Captain, never deserts his bottle or his — (*Hesitates. The captain eyes him sharply.*)

Capt. F. His *flag*, you intended to say, Mr. Moore?

Mr. M. No, Captain. No, sir. I didn't have that in
mind. But it is a very patriotic sentiment. Indeed it is,
sir — yes, sir.

Capt. F. Please excuse me, Mr. Moore; I really
don't —

Mr. M. (*Interrupting.*) No excuses accepted, sir. I
wish to drink your health, sir. (*They fill.*) Captain,

your good health, sir. And I wish for your prosperity and success, sir, — yes, sir.

Capt. F. Thank you, Mr. Moore.

(*They drink. Peter takes glasses, etc. Re-enters the house.*)

Mr. M. Please walk this way, Captain. Those niggers of mine have long ears, Captain. Yes, sir, — long ears, sir.

Capt. F. (*Aside.*) What's this first family man driving at? (*To Mr. M.*) Yes; the African bump of curiosity is generally quite largely developed.

(*They move off the portico towards the seat.*)

Mr. M. Pleasant conceit, Captain. Yes, sir. Do you know, Captain, there is only one animal in the world more curious than the nigger? Yes sir. Only one, sir.

Capt. F. Indeed! (*Aside.*) The old duffer is coming at me with his monkey arguments. I must choke him off.

Mr. M. Yes, sir, — it is the monkey, sir. When I was in —

Capt. F. (*Interrupting.*) Excuse me, Mr. Moore; I don't wish to interrupt you in your cheerful and entertaining narrative of your travels in those tropical countries, — which I think I have heard you say before, you visited in your youthful days.

Mr. M. (*Trying to set in.*) Yes, sir; I —

Capt. F. And — I am always pleased to hear you relate your foreign travels, — I only wish to suggest, that the most inquisitive creature I have ever met is my Lieut. Connery at poker.

Mr. M. Indeed!

Capt. F. Yes; Mr. Moore. He always wishes to know what kind of a hand I have, and whether or not I am bluffing. And let me assure you his inquisitiveness has already cost me my first month's pay; and if he continues in that same frame of mind, he will have my boots and sabre before he gets through. For I can't help bluffing, and he insists on calling me. (*Aside*) I flatter myself I headed off old secesh that time.

Mr. M. (*Aside.*) Good; the poorer the better! (*To Capt. F.*) Yes, sir. Lieut. Connery seems to be a man of great nerve, sir. I should think he might play a strong game, sir. — yes, sir.

Capt. F. You ought to see him play. But I would not advise you to play with him. We are not of the right temperament to meet his game. (*Aside.*) Connery would scoop in this place in a week. Did I understand you to say the ladies were away from home?

Mr. M. Only out for a walk, sir. (*Aside.*) Dern that nigger, why don't he find her? Only out for a walk, sir. And you received my note, sir?

Capt. F. Oh, yes; thank you. And I am obliged to you for your kindness and politeness, Mr. Moore.

Mr. M. Yes, Captain. Thank you, sir. (*They are near the seat. M. feels for papers.*)

Capt. F. (*Aside.*) Why! What's the matter with this old rebel? He don't seem to be drunk, but he is as affable as a candidate for Congress.

Mr. M. Captain, you will excuse me, sir. I am a bluff kind of a man, sir, — yes, sir. It's a way we Southern people have, sir.

Capt. F. (*Aside.*) What the deuce is the matter with old Chivalry?

Mr. M. What I am about to say is sacred, sir — sacred — and I rely on your honor as a gentleman, sir, — on your honor, sir.

Capt. F. Yes; my honor, perhaps, is worth more than my note.

Mr. M. Indeed, Captain, you are a cheerful man, and full of pleasant conceits, sir; and I think a brave man, indeed, — I know it, sir!

Capt. F. (*Aside.*) This is the longest conundrum I ever heard.

Mr. M. But to business sir. I am about to send my daughter South.

(*Captain starts.*)

Capt. F. (*Aside.*) Oh, ho! This wind has a daughterly direction. (*To Mr. Moore.*) Indeed?

Mr. M. Yes, sir; you see, she don't like this business. Your soldiers are offensive. You understand, Captain? Your *soldiers*, not all the officers, sir, — no, sir!

Capt. F. (*Aside.*) I thought so.

Mr. M. She will need a protector, — some one to look after her interests, sir. (*Mr. Moore eyes Captain Fitzhugh*

sharply.   The Captain is amazed.)   But I have though,
sir, considering your relations with the family.   (*Hesitates.*) —

Capt. F.   (*Aside.*)   What in the world have I to do
with his family?

Mr. M.   I have hoped, sir, I could induce you to under-
take the charge, sir, — yes, sir.

Capt. F.   (*Starts. — Aside. — Whistles.*)   Me!   Mr.
Moore?   I go South?   Why, how could I get through the
lines, if I were so disposed?

(*M. produces papers.*)

Mr M.   Here, sir.   Please look at these papers, sir.
(*Hands Capt. Fitzhugh the papers.*)   I am influential with
our people.   These papers fix all that, sir. — yes, sir.

(*Mr. Moore walks away a step or two.*)

Capt. F.   (*Reads.*)   " John Fitzhugh, Brigadier General"— "report for duty"— " Richmond " — " estates in
my trust"— why, Mr. Moore, this comes very unexpect-
edly to me!

Mr. M.   And your answer, Captain.   Here is rank,
wealth, and — Captain, your answer.

Capt. F.   (*Aside.*)   As the Celts say, — " Howly
schmoke!"   (*To M.*)   I wish a little time to consider.

Mr. M.   Certainly, Captain; under ordinary circum-
stances, but in these war times — *Despatch, sir,* — *yes, sir,*
despatch!   You consider this favorably, I hope, sir?

Capt. F.   Mr. Moore, I am a Federal soldier, and —

Mr. M.   I know, sir; but, consider the inducements.

Capt. F.   Yes, Mr. Moore.   I will consider; I will give
you my answer to-morrow.   (*Aside.*)   Will John Fitzhugh desert his family and his colors?   *Hardly!*

Mr. M.   And, Captain!

(*Enter ladies.*)

Bessie.   Captain Fitzhugh, I did not expect to see
you this morning, but I am happy to meet you.

Capt. F.   Thank you, Miss Bessie.   And Miss Eleanor,
have you enjoyed your walk?

Eleanor.   Oh, you have discovered me!   Good morning,
Captain.   So-so; but it is not precisely agreeable to walk

with one who is present in person, while her thoughts are elsewhere. Is it, Captain?

Capt. F. Perhaps not.

Eleanor. Is it, Bessie?

Bessie. (*Pettishly.*) Oh, please stop your nonsense.

(*Re-enter Colonel. The Capt. and the ladies converse on the left centre.*)

Mr. M. Captain, (*Capt. F. moves towards Mr. M.*) please allow me, sir, to present my friend, Colonel Roland. Colonel, this is the Captain of whom you have heard me speak so often,— rescued my daughter, sir. A perfect gentleman, sir,— yes, sir, perfect gentleman.

Col. I am proud to meet you, Captain. Hope you are well, sir. Have heard of you often, sir. How do you like our Southern country, sir?

(*They shake.*)

Capt. F. (*Aside.*) Here is a new first family man. Thank you, Colonel. I am tolerably well. You seem to have a fine country here, sir. A sort of pastoral country, is it not, Colonel? But you don't seem to pan out heavy on sheep. I thought I should be able to procure some of your celebrated Southern South Down mutton, about here, Colonel.

Col. Haven't you had any of our mutton yet, sir?

Capt. F. Can't say that I have, Colonel.

Col. Why, sir, I assure you I have, or I did have, two hundred of the finest sheep you ever saw, sir. But they have disappeared, sir. Yes, sir,— all gone, sir.

Capt. F. Indeed! Disease, Colonel?

Col. No, sir. I reckon not. It's the niggers or the troops, — I don't know which.

Capt. F. Oh! It must be the niggers. The African is fond of sheep, I have heard. And do you know, Colonel, our Northern soldiers come from the cities, mostly, and I doubt if they would dare to look a sheep in the face. Oh no, Colonel. It must be the niggers. I am certain of it.

Col. Mr. Moore, I told you so. Captain —

(*Peter re-enters.*)

Peter (*To Mr. Moore*). Lunch is ready, sah.

Mr. M. All right, Peter.

(*Exit Peter. R. to house. Capt. Fitzhugh offers his arm to Bessie. The Colonel offers his to Eleanor. They move owards the house.*)

Bessie. (*Aside to the Captain.*) Meet me in the grove after lunch without fail.

(*Captain starts.*)

Capt. F. (*Aside to Bessie.*) We will get excused. (*To M.*) Mr. Moore, will you please excuse us from lunch?

Mr. M. Oh, certainly, Captain, if you wish. Yes, sir, — certainly, sir.

(*Bessie and the Captain move to the left. The others to the right, and into the house.*)

Col. (*Aside to M.*) He is fond of that kind of bait.

Mr. M. (*Aside.*) Yes, sir. I have him, sir,— I have him.

(*Scene closes. Flats in front.*)

ACT THIRD.

SCENE SECOND.

(*The grove where Capt. Fitzhugh and Bessie first met. William, the Captain's servant, is discovered looking, as if for some one to the right.*)

William. Not yere? I wonder whar dat Captain can be? Dar's music in de air, — dar is. Rebs 'tack de Yanks. Golly! And whar will dis yere child be?

(*Sings.*)

Oh, ain't I glad I'se out ob de wilderness?
Out ob de wilderness!
Out ob de wilderness!
Oh, ain't I glad I'se out ob de wilderness?
Niggers, bress de Lord!

I wonder whar dat Captain can be; must come dis yere way befo he goes to de camp. Sam Jones says de rebs will 'tack de Captain's camp to-night, shuah! Must tell dis yere to de Captain, befo he sees any odder nigger, shuah! I rudder tink de Captain will make it salubrious for dem rebs. And dat Lieut. Connery — Golly! What a smooth man, dat Massa Connery. Jest as smooth — jest as smooth — till you rubs de fur de wrong way, and den — drap dat cat! drap dat cat! Rebs 'tack dat camp? Go 'way dar, white trash, go 'way dar! (*Discovers the Captain and Bessie approaching. R.*) As shuah as I'se going to be free nigger, dar comes de Captain and young missus Bessie. What's de Captain doing with de young missus? Dar's music yere, for sartain — for sartain. I reckon dis yere child had better leave dis yere place.

(*He hides. Enter Capt. Fitzhugh and Bessie. R.*)

Capt. F. Bessie, it is hard to believe this. I should hardly think my relations — (*hesitates*) — I can hardly believe your father would keep this from me.

(*William listens.*)

Bessie. Captain, you don't quite understand. They all know of your friendly relations with —

(*Checks herself.*)

Capt. F. Hello! what's this?
Bessie. Our family —
Capt. F. (*Aside.*) Oh!
Bessie. And they would not let father into the secret, lest, out of gratitude, he might disclose it to you. And it was not easy, Captain, with all my love for the South and our noble cause, thus to betray our friends. But you once befriended me, and we have met quite often since, and — (*hesitates*) — and I have resolved to befriend you. But if anything should happen to you —
Capt. F. Oh! never fear that. (*Aside.*) Does not this beautiful creature take rather more stock in me than she ought to have in a man with a wife and child?
Bessie. But this will be a desperate fight. And that you should be injured here, so near us — I could not endure that, — no, no!

Capt. F. We shall be prepared for them, Bessie. It will not be especially desperate, I apprehend. (*Aside.*) It is hard to tell where the gratitude leaves off, and the affection begins. Eh?

Bessie. And you will probably capture most of them.

Capt. F. It is my impression now, Bessie, that some of them had better be saving up their money to buy burial caskets if they are particular on that subject. Thirty of them, you say? They attack us at ten; I wish they had concluded to come earlier, so as not to disturb our rest. But I think we will set up for them.

Bessie. Yes, Captain; Colonel Roland's house servant, Sam, followed me about this morning, twenty minutes, to get an opportunity to tell me alone. He didn't dare to go to you for fear of being suspected. He says the leader of the party is now (*William still listens*) at the Colonel's house, and he overheard them talking it over.

· *Capt. F.* You don't mean to say that that dilapidated blonde of a colonel, whom I met at your father's house, is in this thing? Why, he was the politest specimen of the chivalry I have seen. He appeared to be especially solicitous about my health.

Bessie. Captain, please don't speak in that manner of our people. They are brave and chivalrous. But the brave and chivalrous are willing to fight for their country, unless, like my father, they are too old for the service, and it is only such creatures as this Colonel Roland who stay at home and talk fight, while they are cowards at heart, that brings us into disrepute, and leads you Northerners to use the word " chivalry " as a byeword and a reproach. Oh, we have chivalrous men and women, and you will yet meet them. But please excuse me, Captain, as you know I am not usually so patronizing. You know how to act. Don't trouble Colonel Roland or any one at his house,— that would bring suspicion on us at once. But be prepared, Captain, — be ready. (*Hesitates.*) Oh, never mind. Please take me to the house.

Capt. F. Yes, Bessie, I thank you for great kindness and consideration. I know I ought not to have spoken as I did just now; but I am not a saint, and —

(*They move off. R.*)

5

Bessie. There, Captain! Please say no more about it.
Capt. F. Yes. But that blonde Col —

(*Exeunt. R. William comes from his hiding place.*)

Wm. If dat nigger, Sam Jones, hasn't done gone tell de young missus — I'se a nigger sinner. Dar's going to be music round about yere. Thirty rebs going for de Yanks. I reckon dat camp is no place for dis yere child. Rebs 'tack de Yanks! Go way dar, white trash! Go way, dar! (*Sings.*) But —

> I lubs to hear the breezes a kissing in de lane,
> I lubs to see de old folks when I've get home again;
> I lubs to hear the breezes a humming all de day,—
> But de sweetest ting I eber saw,
> Was my sweet Sally Gray.

(*Shuffles.*)

> Oh, Sally Gray, she looks so gay,
> I really tink I will;
> Oh, Sally Gray, she looks so gay,
> Keep still, me heart, keep still!
> Oh, Sally Gray, she looks so gay,
> I really tink I will;
> Oh, Sally Gray, she looks so gay,
> Keep still, me heart, keep still!

(*Exits. L.*)

(*Scene Closes.*)

ACT THIRD.

SCENE THIRD.

(*Camp, same as before. Time, half-past nine, P. M. Moon dimly seen through the clouds. The piece of artillery off,— sentry as before,— a bright fire in the middle of the stage. The tents are lighted. In the officers' tent, Capt. Fitzhugh and Lieut. Morgan smoking,— Morgan reads a paper by the light of a candle stuck in a bottle. As the curtain rises, enter soldier with mail-bags, from L. He moves to Sergt. Thompson's quarters.*)

Sol. Mail, Sergeant!

Sergt. T. Turn out for mail! Turn out for mail! (*Men rush to the Sergeant's tent for letters.*) Come! Steady there, men!

(*They gradually disperse — some with letters — to their quarters.*)

Capt. F. Mr. Morgan, didn't you hear some one say mail?

Lieut. Morgan. Yes, sir; I thought so.

Capt. F. Rather late, to-night; but it is because we are so far from the main camp.

(*A soldier moves from the Sergeant's tent to the Captain's with a small package, such as could be sent by mail, and two letters.*)

Sol. (*To Capt. Fitzhugh.*) Mail, sir.

Capt. F. Come in.

(*The soldier (Orderly) leaves the mail-matter with the Captain, and moves back to his quarters, saluting at entrance and exit.*)

Capt. F. A letter from home, — good!

Lieut. Morgan. And one for me, — better!

Capt F. Better for you, you mean, Mr. Morgan.

Lieut. Morgan. Oh, yes, sir.

(*They read. The package is for the Captain, and contains a photograph of his wife and child. He moves to the camp-fire to look at it. Lieut. Morgan remains in his quarters reading.*)

Capt. F. (*Aside with emotion.*) A picture of my wife and child! Such a coincidence! She did not write me of this. And here I am, hardly out of that old rebel's sight and hearing, who talked to me of promotion and wealth, and —— Be —— his daughter. (*Looks at it again; then at his uniform, forcibly.*) I pass! That blonde Colonel, however, must be salted. He won't make a handsome corpse. But what's the use of being particular among friends? (*To his tent. To Mr. M.*) No bad news, I hope, Mr. Morgan.

Lieut. Morgan. Well, no sir; not absolutely bad. But my poor mother writes very despondently.

Capt. F. Sorry to hear that, sir. It is the worst feature of this war, the sadness and gloom it brings, like a cold fog about our homes. You will hardly write her to-night; perhaps not until after this scrimmage is over.

Lieut. Morgan. I think I will write a word to-night, Captain, and leave it to be sent to-morrow, if anything happens to me. I have a presentiment I shall catch it to-night.

Capt. F. Oh no, Mr. Morgan. Of course, you can write, if you see fit. But this will be a one-sided affair. They don't know we are expecting them, and we will gun them as boys shoot chickens in the country barnyards. Why, Mr. Morgan, I feel now, as if the mine had not been discovered which is to furnish the lead for the bullet to shoot me.

Lieut. Morgan. Yes; I know you are a cheerful man, Captain, but I —

Capt. F. (*Interrupting.*) Oh, no! Here, take a trifle of the army contractors' ready relief! (*Proffers him a canteen.*)

Lieut. Morgan. No, thank you, Captain.

Capt. F. No; but I think I will press my peppermint. (*The Capt. drinks. Morgan writes.*) Sergeant?

(*Sergeant appears. Left and rear.*)

Sergt. T. Here, sir!

Capt. F. Mr. Connery has not yet returned.

Sergt. T. He will be due in about twenty minutes.

Capt F. Yes. Sergeant, come in. (*Sergeant enters the tent.*) Sergeant, we are to be attacked to-night. And, Sergeant, this is not a false alarm. Have you any rope in camp?

Sergt. T. Yes, sir; we have about fifty feet of half-inch rope which they left from the forage wagons, when they brought the straw.

Capt. F. Well, Sergeant. I wish you to loosen all the guy-ropes on this side of the tents. (*Points to the side.*) Do you understand, Sergeant?

Sergt. T. Yes, sir.

Capt. F. And fasten the ropes to each of the tents, to extend as far as possible from them, so that at signal the tents can be pulled down instantly, and the camp left clear for gunning purposes. We are going to have a shooting match in this camp. Do you comprehend, Sergeant?

Sergt. T. I think so, sir.

Capt. F. Have your men pack their knapsacks and take them to the hill over there, and have them ready to withdraw with their pieces and fifty rounds of ammunition. Instruct the picket up the pike to see nobody, and not to allow himself to be taken without giving any alarm; and the same with the camp-guard, and keep up a good camp-fire. Do you understand, Sergeant?

Sergt. T. Perfectly, sir.

Capt. F. Have you seen my boy, William, this evening, Sergeant?

Sergt. T. No, sir. I don't think he is in camp.

Capt. F. Perhaps that intelligent and discreet citizen has got wind of this. Dismissed. (*The Sergeant salutes and retires up.*) Mr. Morgan, if we are not able to bag the most of these Johnnies on that plan, our pay ought to be stopped.

(*The Sergeant instructs the sentry, as he passes to his quarters — but does not speak so as to be heard. The men are seen moving about, making preparations. Enter Lieut. Connery, with squad from picket. R. Connery moves directly to his quarters. The squad moves to the men's quarters; the Sergt. in command.*)

Sergt. Squad, halt! By the right flank, right face! Break ranks, march!

(*They disperse.*)

Lieut. Connery. (*To the Captain.*) Well, Captain, (*lights his pipe*) what's up? Good evening, Mr. Morgan.

Lieut. Morgan. Good evening, Mr. Connery.

Capt. F. What's up? Not much. But somebody is liable to be *down* before morning. A party of guerillas proposes to surprise this camp to-night. That's all.

Lieut. Connery. Yes? Is not that dodge pretty much played out?

5*

Capt. F. Well, it seems not. It has not been played at all yet.

Lieut. Connery. But it has been threatened often enough.

(*Begins to remove his coat and sabre.*)

Capt. F. Oh, you need not unharness yet. This is a go, certain. They visit us at ten, or thereabouts, — I know it.

Lieut. Connery. Yes? How do you know it?

Capt. F. My gentle tiger, please excuse me from answering that question, although it is not leading (*Capt. F. begins to put on his coat and sabre*), for it involves private domestic relations.

Lieut. Connery. Yes? Petticoats?

Capt F. Yes, petticoats, and possibly duplex elliptics, — old man. This is to be one of the times that try men's souls. Mine don't fully satisfy me, but I think I will stay by and see it out. I will explain in detail, presently. Orderly!

(*Orderly enters.*)

Orderly. Here, sir!

Capt. F. Tell the 1st Sergeant to have taps blown.

(*Orderly moves to 1st Sergeant Thompson's tent.*)

1st Sergeant. Bugler, blow taps!

(*Taps blown — bugler need not be seen. He uses the Artillery call for taps. Stage should be perfectly silent while this is going on. Lights out.*)

Sentry. Lights out!

(*Lights disappear through the camp. Captain F. picks up Lieut. Connery's or Lieut Morgan's cap, and uses it as a snuffer to extinguish candle.*)

Capt. F. (*Softly.*) Sergeant Thompson?

Sergt. T. (*Softly.*) Here, sir.

(*The camp is now very quiet, and all conversation is in a low tone.*)

Capt. F. Ropes adjusted?

Sergt. T. Yes, sir.

Capt. F. Picket and guard instructed?

Sergt. T. Yes, sir.

Capt. F. Form the company!

Sergt. T. Yes, sir.

(*The Sergt. moves to the tents, looks in — as if calling out the men, but does not speak so as to be heard. The company forms quietly and silently. Officers stand whispering together.*)

(*To Capt.*) Company is formed, sir!

Capt. F. Thank you, Sergeant. (*Officers in proper places — softly.*) Company! By the right flank, right face! Forward by file right, march!

(*The company moves off to the left and rear — disappears. Part of the command remains with Capt. Fitzhugh, and Lieut. Morgan on the left, and the rest, about one-third, with Lieut. Connery, crosses over by the rear of the stage, so as not to be seen, to the right. Enter William, R. William moves to Capt's. tent.*)

William. (*To Sentry.*) Mr. Soger, whar is de Captain?

Sentry. What do you want of him, moak?

William. De rebs am a coming, shuah!

Sentry. Well, let 'em come! I ain't going to kick, — I ain't! The Captain is with the company on the hill, over there. You better git out of this. They will make a stiff of you, — they will.

William. Oh, I don't fear nuffin! I'se been watching dem rebs dese two hours. Golly! Won't dey cotch it?

(*Exit L.*)

(*A short interval. Suddenly, about a dozen musket shots are fired into the camp from the attacking party on the RIGHT, but the party is not seen from the front. The sentry falls, as if he were shot; taking care to have his musket near by; his face to the REAR of the stage, — Federals quite silent, and unseen. THEN, six or eight heads are seen pushed out from the right, and quickly withdrawn. Then, enter Col. Roland.*)

Colonel. (*Softly.*) This way, gentlemen! (*To Captain's tent.*) Our game is here. (*Finds tent empty.*) Some derned Yankee game!

(*He is followed by a crowd of men, as many as can be fur-
nished, up to twenty-five or thirty, in all sorts of costumes,
and a few gray uniforms. They peer about the tents,
and one approaches Scot, the sentry, and empties his
pockets,* KNEELING ON HIM *while he does it. Another
pulls off Scot's boots, or attempts it. As* SOON *as the attacking party is well on, the tents are* QUICKLY PULLED OVER,
*and the stage cleared. Light is gradually thrown on the
middle of the stage, but not too much of it.*)

Rebel officer. Now then, men, stand by!

(*The men cluster about him in no particular order, with their
pieces ready for action, looking in all directions.*)

Capt. F. (*Outside, loudly.*) Company, ready! Aim!
Fire! (*They fire. Several of the attacking party drop, and
the others face in the direction of the firing.*) How are you,
chivalry? Charge!

(*Fitzhugh's men should be so posted as to show the blaze of
their muskets to the audience, and at the command
" charge!" they commence to cheer and yell. But they
must not come on too quickly for they are supposed to come
some little distance.*)

Rebel officer. Stand up to them, men! Ready! Aim!
Fire! (*They fire on Capt. Fitzhugh's party before they get
in sight from the front.*) Stand firm, men!

(*They rally about him at " charge bayonets."*)

Capt. F. Rally, men, rally! Give them your steel!
Go for them!

(*Capt. Fitzhugh's party charges down on the attacking
party from the left. The attacking party pours in their*
RESERVED *fire. Several of F's. men drop, including Lieut.
Morgan. Attacking party stands firm. Capt. Fitzhugh's
party* RETIRES. *The attacking party at this, cheer wildly,
and yell.*)

Capt. F. (*Outside on left.*) Steady, there, men! Get
into line! Dress up on the left, there! Now, go for them
again! Charge!

*(The attacking party in the meantime is reloading. Capt.
Fitzhugh's party again moves on the attacking party in the
centre of the stage with cheers and yells. The last yield;
they fall back nearer the right. Capt. Fitzhugh's men
give fresh cheers, and just then Lieut. Connery with his
men dashes out from the right and the rear on the attacking party.)*

Lieut. Connery. Surrender, you lousy rascals! Drop
your pieces and down on your knees! (*They throw down
their pieces, some drop on their knees, others throw up their
arms in token of surrender.*)

Capt. F. Look out there, Mr. Connery! You are los-
ing your temper.

Lieut. Connery. Yes, I came near it.

Colonel. (*Rising, picks up a musket and aims at Capt.
Fitzhugh.*) Here goes one for luck!

Sergeant. (*Rising, shoots the Colonel, just as Lieut.
Connery jumps at him.*) Yes! And here goes another for
fun. (*Several Federals make for the Colonel's pockets.
William steps up to Capt. F. and offers him a canteen.
The men cheer and yell. William shuffles.*)

(*Curtain down.*)

ACT FOURTH.

SCENE FIRST.

(*Capt. Fitzhugh's winter quarters, — two years having elapsed since last Act. Log hut, — the logs being squared on three sides, so as to present an even appearance inside; the rough, or natural part of the logs being outside. It runs across the stage from right to left, and is large and capacious. The walls are about ten feet high; the rafters are of* PLANK, *covered with* CANVAS *for a roof. In the middle, there is a chimney of brick, with a large fire-place; a board mantle over the fire-place; with cigar-boxes, pipes, &c., thereon. On the* RIGHT *of the chimney, a door leading into a cook room; and there are doors in both ends. There are three camp bedsteads, with blankets, &c., thereon, — leather pillows, or rubber pillows. On the walls hang three sabres, pistols, sashes, belts, &c., (equipments). There is a water-bucket of leather (old-fashioned fire-bucket, contributed by some Virginia household), and there is a rude set of shelves with tin dippers and pewter mugs, one or two common bottles — bitter bottles, &c., — a demijohn near by. In the middle, a long pine table, with one or two newspapers, books of tactics, and of the gospel, thereon, and a cribbage-board. Capt. Fitzhugh and Lieut. Thompson are playing cribbage.*)

Capt. F. See here! Mr. Thompson, it seems to me you are pegging quite lively. Thompson, were you a shoemaker when you enlisted?

Lieut. Thompson. No, sir. But I hope to last long enough to get as much promotion as some of the shoe-makers are getting.

(*They play.*)

Capt. F. Six.

Lieut. Thompson. And nine are fifteen, — two holes.

Capt F. Take 'em, and look cheerful.

Lieut. Thompson. And eight — twenty-three, and eight, is a pair, two holes — (*pegs*) and thirty-one, two holes more,— and last card another hole. (*Pegs.*)

Capt. F. How's that, Thompson?

Lieut. Thompson. Oh, that's all right, Captain. The two eights make a pair, don't they?

Capt. F. Certainly.

Lieut. Thompson. And my eight on your twenty-three makes thirty-one,— two holes more.

Capt. F. So you say.

Lieut. Thompson. And last card, another hole,— five in all. Oh, it's all right, Captain. I will leave it to Connery, for the drinks.

Capt. F. Yes; out of my demijohn! See here, Thompson! Since you came into our mess, I have lost more than a million of dollars in leaving your bets to Connery. That's played out; and if I catch you cheating, I will send you on picket duty, once a week *extra*, all winter. (*Rap outside.*) Come in!

(*Enter Orderly. R.*)

Orderly. A gentleman outside wishes to see you, Captain!

Capt. F. What does he look like?

Orderly. Biled shirt.

Capt. F. Send him in.

(*Exit Orderly. R.*)

Capt. F. I reckon we will see him, eh, **Mr.** Thompson, if it don't cost too much? But it may be one of those tract scatterers. Shove those (the cards), out of sight! Cover that demijohn, and get out the Bible!

(*They arrange matters. Enter the Hon. Samuel Blowhard, R.*)

Capt. F. (*Aside.*) A chaplain from civil life. (*To B.*) How do you do, sir?

Blowhard. Capt. Fitzhugh, I suppose?

Capt. F. Yes, sir. I have been laboring under that same impression for about forty years.

Blowhard. Captain, my name is Blowhard. I am the member from your district, — Samuel Blowhard.

Capt. F. Yes, sir. I am happy to see you here, sir! Member of Congress, I understood you to say?

Blowhard. Yes, sir. Member of the house of representatives.

Capt. F. Indeed! Won't you be seated? (*Aside.*) Thompson, get out the demijohn and cover up the Bible. I am truly happy to meet you here, Mr. Blowup.

Blowhard. Blowhard, Captain. If you please, — Samuel Blowhard!

Capt. F. Excuse me, sir. When did you leave Washington?

Blowhard. Yesterday, Captain, — and I had a terrible time of it in getting here.

Capt. F. Indeed! I wonder at that. A civilian generally receives great attention in the army.

Blowhard. Oh! I received attention enough, I assure you, Captain, — the loss of all my carpet-bag contained proves that.

Capt. F. Yes, Mr. Blowhard. There are so many servants in the army who are given to petit larceny, that — do you ever take anything, sir? I mean to drink. Please excuse me for asking. I had an idea that congressmen never took anything (*aside*), except their pay. We have a little commissary.

(*Thompson exits quietly, L.*)

Blowhard. Yes, Captain. Thank you. I will try it.

Capt F. Oh, yes. (*Loudly.*) Fire! Fire!

Blowhard. Captain! Fire? Where?

Capt. F. Oh, I didn't think. You see, Mr. Blowhard, that's my way of calling William when we drink. I take that way to let him know the nature of the duty he is wanted for. He usually comes very lively on that call, for he frequently manages to get a drink out of it.

(*Enter William, from cook-room.*)

William. Yere I is, sah.

(*William without any other order moves directly to the water buckets and proceeds to help them.*)

Blowhard. (*To Capt. F.*) Intelligent man, Captain.

William. (*To Blowhard.*) Water, sah?

Capt. F. Oh, yes, he comes from one of the first families on his father's side.

William. (*To Capt. F.*) Water, sah?

Capt. F. (*To Blowhard, who is quite bald.*) Mr. Blowhard; here's the hair all off the top of your head. Please excuse me, sir. I did not notice your infirmity, for you look like a younger man, generally. That's our regular toast. It's a way we have of expressing the hope, that our friends may live long enough to be compelled to use store hair.

Blowhard. Oh, it is? I see much in the army that is entirely new to me. Thank you, Captain. (*They drink. William takes the utensils to the shelves and steals a drink. Exit cook-room.*) So, Captain, these are your winter quarters.

Capt. F. Yes, sir. Here is where we poor fellows suffer during the winter months. It is awful, sir! (*Aside.*) He will think so if Connery strikes him at poker.

Blowhard. It is wonderful! (*Looks about.*) And you seem to have another room out there?

(*Pointing to C. R. door.*)

Capt. F. Yes, sir. We think this will do; our men whacked this up in three days on only six extra rations of commissary. The bricks for that chimney we borrowed of one of our neigbors, who had previously loaned the army the other parts of his family mansion. In there? That is our cook-room and servants' hall. My boy William holds a town meeting in there from the time we turn in in the evening, until we turn out, in the morning, at which latter time he usually commences to sleep.

Blowhard. You don't mean to say you have a cook?

Capt. F. Don't I? Here. Uncle Peter! Uncle Peter!

(*Enter Peter, C. R. This must be a venerable nigger, with a hitch in his gait, and the other boy, William, by disguising, can play the part.*)

Uncle Peter. Dat's me!

(He bows incessantly, but says nothing.)

Capt. F. Don't that look like a cook?

Blowhard. Well, I declare!

Capt. F. Uncle Peter, — how old are you?

Uncle Peter. Two hundred and twelve years, massa Captain.

(Bows and scrapes. B. laughs.)

Capt. F. How long have you been cooking, uncle?

Uncle Peter. Free hundred and nine years, massa Captain.

(B. laughs.)

Capt. F. Uncle Peter. This gentleman is just from Washington, — he is a member of Congress, uncle.

(Peter starts, bows, and scrapes.)

Uncle Peter. What! *(Aside.)* Looks like de sutler! Is you one ob de gemmen what gibs out de bureaus? Cos if you is, I wants one wid a looking-glass.

(All laugh)

Capt. F. Oh, never mind that bureau now, uncle.

Uncle Peter. No, sah! Just as you say, massa Captain.

Capt. F. Just give us one verse, uncle, and then give us our dinner.

Uncle Peter. Massa Captain, indeed I will.

(Sings.)

I am de jolliest cullud pusson eber you did see,
What's trabelled troo dis wicked world and seen fo' sco' and free,
And nebber lay down;
And my name am Peter Brown.
And tho' I'm getting gray,
I feel just like I used to feel,
When in my younger days,
And nebber lay down.

(Shuffles to C. R. door.)

And nebber lay down.
And nebber lay down.
And my name am Peter Brown.
And tho' I'm getting gray,
I feel just like I used to feel,
When in my younger days

(Outside.)

And nebber lay down.
And nebber lay down.

Blowhard. A very interesting old man, sir. I thought you had to do your own cooking, Captain?

Capt. F. Yes, sir; I know that is the popular notion about soldiering. And I remember to have seen a play in which there was a scene representing several British officers in the Crimea, who were, by the way, of the British aristocracy, doing their own cooking; which is doubtless a very common practice among the officers of the English aristocracy; but it is *not* popular with us free-born Americans. We grub it sometimes on the march, but as cooks in camp we don't excel — any to speak of.

(*Enter Lieuts. Connery and Thompson.*)

Mr. Blowhard: these are my officers; this is Lieut Connery, and this Lieut. Thompson. Mr. Blowhard, gentlemen, member of Congress from our district.

(*They shake.*)

Mr. B. Happy to meet you, gentlemen.

Lieut. Thompson. Thank you, sir.

Lieut. Connery. Yes, house or senate, sir?

Blowhard. House of representatives, Mr. Connery.

Lieut. Connery. Yes; I hope you will enjoy yourself here.

(*C. moves off, eyeing Blowhard. Lieut. Thompson goes for a pipe.*)

B'owhard. Captain, I thought you had an officer, Morgan, by name?

Capt. F. Oh, yes, sir! we did have; but we left poor Morgan in a guerilla fight early in the war.

Blowhard. Indeed! I do not remember to have seen his death announced in the papers.

Lieut. Connery. Probably they spelt it *Mush,* or anything but Morgan, so that it escaped your notice, Mr. Blowhard.

Blowhard. Possibly, sir.

Capt. F. Yes, sir. We have not yet had much opportunity for promotion, for they kept us in the defences of Washington until the last fall. But the spring campaign bids fair to offer right smart of promotion. Eh, Connery?

Lieut. Connery. Yes! I expect to be the captain of this company by the next fourth of July.

Blowhard. But what is to become of the captain?

Capt. F. Oh, I am going up!

Lieut. Connery. Yes, — or down! (*Pointing to the floor. Aside to Capt.*) I wish to see you alone.

Capt. F. (*Aside.*) All right. (*Captain nods to Lieut. Thompson. They approach. Blowhard is looking at the arms, etc.*) (*Aside to T*) Take him in to dinner, please; I want to speak with Connery. (*To B.*) Mr. Blowhard, it is nearly dinner time. Perhaps you would like a drop of bitters.

Blowhard. Well, sir; I don't mind. (*Aside.*) I'm nearly famished.

Capt. F. (*Loudly.*) Fire! Fire!

(*Re-enter William C. R. William moves directly to water bucket as before. They fill.*)

Blowhard. Your healths, gentlemen.

(*They nod and drink, and William puts away utensils and steals another drink.*)

Capt. F. William, ask Uncle Peter how long it will be before he can give us our dinner?

William. Yes, sah!

(*He re-enters cook room.*)

Capt. F. You will not find our dinner very elaborate, Mr. Blowhard; but solid and substantial, I trust.

(*Re-enter William, C. R.*)

William. Dinner is ready, sah.

Capt. F. Mr. Blowhard, please walk in with Mr. Thompson; and I must ask you to excuse Mr. Connery and myself for a short time. He has just returned from a court martial, and I wish to talk over a little court business.

Blowhard. Certainly, Captain!

Lieut. Thompson. This way, if you please, sir!

(*They enter cook-room. William follows.*)

Capt. F. Mr. Connery, — what's up?

Lieut. Connery. **Yes!** You know Captain, we have been trying that prisoner Eaton, whom we took on the picket line.

Capt. F. Yes, -- as a spy.

Lieut. Connery. Yes; and although, as you know, Captain, I have no right to disclose the findings of the court, I will in this case; for I don't believe he was here as a spy, but was only trying to get North to visit his friends. He was found guilty and sentenced to be hung.

Capt. F. Well, old man, how does this properly affect my dinner?

Lieut. Connery. Yes, dinner! After the trial was over, he sent for me, and asked me if I knew *you!*

Capt. F. Me!

(*Starts.*)

Lieut. Connery. Yes, and when I told him I was one of your officers, he told me his story. It was just what I suspected; but there was no other lawyer on the court detail, and it is a case of rope, — so far. He gave me this.

(*Lieut. Connery hands the Captain a paper. The Captain starts and reads.*)

Capt. F. " *I am not a spy. Perhaps you have heard of me. Clarence King.*" Good Heavens! Connery! This is the affianced lover of Be——, — of the lady who gave us information of the guerilla attack.

Lieut. Connery. Yes, I thought so.

Capt. F. Connery, please go in; make some excuse to that M. C., and get him out here; and keep Thompson in there while I talk with the public benefactor. I never before thought a member of Congress could be of any earthly use; but I have changed my mind.

Lieut. Connery. Yes, certainly, Captain.

(*Lieut. Connery enters cook-room*)

Capt. F. Clarence King — Bessie Moore's lover, appeals to me. Hang him! Quartermaster, you need *not* make a requisition for that rope. (*Enter Blowhard, from cook-room.*) Mr. Blowhard, please excuse me, sir, for interrupting you at dinner; but it is a case of life and death.

Blowhard. Captain!

6*

Capt. F. Yes, sir! Perhaps you have heard of our scrimmage with the guerillas, where we were saved through the information of a lady?

Blowhard. I think I *did* hear of it. There was a lady in the case if I remember correctly. Rather romantic, was it not?

Capt. F. Very romantic, and exceedingly convenient. Now, sir, a confederate officer to whom that lady is engaged, has been arrested, tried, and convicted as a spy, and sentenced to be hung. The findings of the court are on the way to Washington by this time, and I wish to save him, — to have him pardoned.

Blowhard. But suppose he really were a spy?

Capt. F. But he was not! I —

Blowhard. Excuse me; he has been convicted as such.

Capt. F. Mr. Blowhard, I care not if he were a spy! His future wife, if we can save him, once saved my life, and perhaps the lives of most of our company. Now, I propose to save him, *guilty or not guilty!* Will you assist me?

Blowhard. Well, Captain, you seem to take this so much at heart, I think we will see what can be done.

Capt. F. Thank you, Mr. Blowhard. (*Takes his hand.*) God bless you! Go in and finish your dinner. I am off to head-quarters for a leave of absence, and then to one of my battery friends for horses — we must start to-night — to-night, Mr. Blowhard.

Blowhard. But, Captain, it is a ride of fifty miles!

Capt. F. And it is a case of life and death!

Blowhard. (*Hesitating.*) I will go.

Capt. F. Good!

(*Mr. Blowhard to cook-room. Capt. F. to right door.*)
Clarence, my boy, I will save thee!

(*Scene closes. Flats in front.*)

ACT FOURTH.

SCENE SECOND.

(*A wood in Virginia. Thin growth of maple, cedar, oak and hemlock trees.*)

(*Enter Capt. Fitzhugh.*)

Capt. F. If that M. C. didn't turn up just in time! What a coincidence! Bessie Moore saved me from these blood-thirsty guerillas, and *now* I am to save her lover, Clarence King, from the gallows. Stand a man on a caisson, tie a rope about his neck, fasten the other end to a tree, and then move on the caisson and leave him to struggle with the rope, — ugh! It's bad enough to stand up and take your chance of being shot for the politicians of your country; but I don't think it would be sweet to die for one's country on the end of a rope. Clarence, my boy, you shall have a chance of getting winged, and become an experimental subject for some youthful medical student. (*He discovers Mr. B. and William approaching.*) Hello! who is this?

(*Enter Blowhard and William. William has a lantern. L.*)

Blowhard. Captain — you here? on your way back to camp, I suppose?

Capt. F. Yes, sir. I have the leave and the horses.

Blowhard. I am so glad you have been so successful. I thought I ought not to leave camp without calling on your Colonel, and I asked William to show me over. The Colonel don't live in my district, but he is a very influential man in an adjoining district.

Capt. F. Certainly — I go in for influential men, *strong* just now. I suppose you know acres of those people in Washington. Do you wish anything more of William, sir? I will accompany you to the Colonel's quarters.

Blowhard. Oh, no. He only came to direct me.

Capt. F. William, you can return to camp, and you can take the lantern with you ; we can get on better without it. Come, Mr. Blowhard, if you please.

(*Exeunt. R.*)

William. Yes, sah, I ken go back to de camp — but dar is suffing goin on yere, dar is ; mighty curious child, dis yere — mighty curious. (*Discovers some one coming.*) What! Why, bress me, if dar isn't a white trash! (*Enter poor Virginia farmer from L. William holds lantern* FULL *in his face.*) Who is yer, Mister?

Farmer. Whose nigger are you?

William. See here, white trash. I don't want none of yer tobacco field talk, — dat's played out. I'se one of Uncle Sam's boys, — I is. Squit yer lip music! Squit yer nonsense, old rebellion.

Farmer. (*Aside.*) The insolence of these niggers, when the Federals are about! But there may be a regiment near by.

William. (*Aside.*) What's dat bacon-and-greens trash muttering about?

Farmer. My good man —

William. Dar it is! Dat's de way you all talk when de Yanks am yere.

Farmer. But, my good man, can you tell me where the sutler is?

William. Looking for de sutler, is yer? Werry bad time dis yere for you folks to be looking for de sutler. Got a pass? Got any money?

Farmer. (*Nervously.*) I have only a little confederate money, my good man.

William. What! Confederate money!

Farmer. No ; I mean greenbacks, — a small amount of greenbacks to buy a few stores for my family. (*Aside.*) I believe this nigger means to rob me.

William. See yere! Old brick dust! De sutler's tent am a right smart ways down dar, and you better be getting ; for if any ob our boys finds you yere, dey will clean you out, — do you hear?

Farmer. Yes ; I hear ; I'm going. Good evening, my good man, good evening.

(*Exit R.*)

William. Dat's played. Git! Git dar, Johnny! Dese yere white trash am mighty good when de Yanks am yere; but when de rebs come, — git dar, nigger! Git! (*William moves towards left.*) What's dis yere.

(*Hides.*)

(*Enter a squad of soldiery, a corporal and four men. Between the men marches Clarence King. — William watches.*)

William. If dat was not Massa King, I neber see him befo. Whar is dey going?

(*The soldiers move directly across the stage without halting, and off at the right.*)

William. Whar is dey going wid Massa Clarence?

(*William follows. Scene closes. Flats open.*)

ACT FOURTH.

SCENE THIRD.

(*Head-quarters of Col. McManus. Ten days have elapsed since last scene. On the RIGHT a poor Virginia planter's house of squared logs, whitewashed, with broad portico, one story and a half high. Locust trees about on the LEFT; two or three officers' wall tents. It is in the evening; a sentry in an overcoat, paces in front, and there is a bright camp fire burning in the middle, about half-way back. Enter Col. McManus from house to portico.*)

Colonel. Sentry! Has Mr. Connery sent me another orderly?

Sentry. No, sir. But Mr. Connery is in the adjutant's quarters.

Colonel. (*Loudly.*) Mr. Connery!

(*Connery appears from officers' tent.*)

Lieut. Connery. Yes, Colonel!

Colonel. Excuse me. Mr. Connery, for calling you out, but my boots are off. How about that orderly?

Lieut. Connery. Yes, Colonel. The Sergeant made another detail before I left camp. Scot, who was on duty here, was taken sick.

Colonel. Sick, or drunk?

Lieut. Connery. Yes, a little of both, perhaps. (*Aside*) But I don't understand it — here at head-quarters. Something is up! But here comes the Sergeant, now, sir.

(*Enter Sergt. Harding, R. With him, Bessie Moore, disguised as a* FEDERAL SOLDIER, — PRIVATE MILROY. *This disguise must be* PERFECT. *None of those fancy, big-hipped, lady-like soldiers, but a Federal soldier in the proper uniform; and, as it is in the night-time, he can wear an overcoat.*)

Sergt. H. (*Salutes.*) Detail for orderly, sir.

Colonel. All right. Sergeant dismissed.

(*Exit R. Lieut. Connery scrutinizes Milroy.*)

Colonel. Have you done any orderly duty, my man?

Milroy. (*Salutes.*) Only at company head-quarters, sir.

Colonel. It is the same here. Make yourself comfortable where you can hear me when I call.

(*Colonel re-enters house.*)

Lieut. Connery. Where have I seen that face before?

(*Lieut. Connery re-enters officers' quarters. Milroy saunters about, looking here and there.*)

Sentry. Say, old pal; just jined?

Milroy. I joined two days since.

Sentry. Then you must have a chaw about yer.

Milroy. Certainly.

(*Proffers sentry tobacco.*)

Sentry. That's none of yer sutler's plug, is it?

Milroy. Oh, no! I bought it in Washington, on my way here. (*Looks about.*) Would you like a drink?

Sentry. You bet! Got any? (*Milroy nods*) Go out there, where it is darker. Some bloody smeller may be round. (*They move well to left; he drinks.*) That's good for the chills : got that in Washington, too, old pal?

Milroy. Yes !

Sentry. I thought so.

(*He paces. Milroy moves as far as possible from the sentry to the left. Sentry keeps well to the right*)

Milroy. (*Aside.*) So far I have been fortunate, indeed. I had some little difficulty in getting into this regiment, but luckily they were in need of recruits. But I was terribly scared when I was detailed into Capt. Fitzhugh's company ; and how fortunate for me that the Captain is absent on leave. I don't think this disguise, even, would deceive him ; for Lieut. Connery, who never saw me but once, has been watching me sharply. What if they detect me ! Oh, Clarence ! Clarence ! how much I love thee ! But the papers ! To find the papers !

Sentry. Say, old pal ! what are you doing out there?

Milroy. Oh, nothing, — I'm only thinking.

Sentry. Kind of lonesome? Oh, you will get use to it.

Milroy. Yes ; I think so. (*Aside.*) That is the office tent. (*Loud laughter and noise in the office tent.*) The papers must be in there. But how to get at them. Those officers seem likely to make a night of it. Hear them. They little know, and for that matter, perhaps, little care, for the misery and sufferings of others. And Clarence is in irons almost within hearing of their carousal. Oh, this war ! This horrid, cruel war ! But the papers ! Those fearful papers, condemning my Clarence to be hung like a dog. (*Shudders.*) Let me but find them, and destroy them, and it will give our friends time to work for his pardon, and then to escape from this, before the Captain returns.

(*Colonel comes from the house to the portico.*)

Col. Orderly !

Milroy. Here, sir !

Col. Take these papers to brigade head-quarters. Do you know where they are?

Milroy. Oh yes, sir !

(*Takes the papers. Colonel re-enters the house.*)

Milroy. (*To sentry.*) Please tell me where the brigade head-quarters are?

Sentry. (*Laughs.*) Oh, just across there, old pal. That big Sibley tent is where you want to go.

(*M. moves off, R., looking at the papers.*)

Milroy. What if the papers were here!

(*Exit R.*)

Sentry. Blow me, if that isn't the gamest cove I ever see; didn't know where he was going, and wouldn't ask old Mc. (*Enter William, L.*) Say, Moak; haven't a chaw, have yer?

William. Course, I has; as de Captain says, I am fond of the critter comforts.

(*Proffers sentry tobacco.*)

Sentry. Good boy, Moak. You are going to vote, you are.

William. Yes, sah! Soger, you hasn't seen nuffin of dem odder niggers, has yer?

Sentry. Oh, yes! They are in the kitchen, they are.

William. I'll go in dar. (*Moves off, as if to go in the rear of the house on the right, suddenly turns to the left.*) (*Aside.*) I wonder whar dat massa King can be. About yere somewhere, shuah! He is de man what dey tried for de spy. Hang dat massa King! De debil dey will.

(*Exit L. Re-enter Milroy, R.*)

Milroy. Not among those, surely. (*Noise in the office tent.*) Will they ever vacate that tent?

William. (*Outside, loudly.*) Help, dar! Help, dar! Come out yere some ob you niggers! (*William rushes on, L.*) Where dose niggers? (*Discovers Milroy.*) Here, soger! Come out yere, if you please! Dar is an officer has fell down dar, and de man is done gone killed. Come out yere. Mr. Soger, if you please!

(*William retreats, and is followed by Milroy. They bring in Capt. Fitzhugh, who is insensible; when they get near the camp fire William recognizes the Captain.*)

William. Oh, golly, soger! It's de massa Captain! It's de massa Captain!

(*Milroy stands confounded.*)

(*Connery rushes out of the office tent*)

Lieut. Connery. William, what's the matter here? Whom have you there? (*Recognizes the Captain.*) Good Heavens! it's the Captain! Bring him in here. (*Lieut. Connery takes the Captain by the shoulders.*) Lay hold of his feet there, my man! You look as if you were petrified!

(*All take hold, and carry him in. William rushes out of the tent.*)

William. De doctor! whar am de doctor?

(*Exit L. Milroy comes from the tent.*)

Milroy. Capt. Fitzhugh here! and hurt! perhaps fatally. His horse must have fallen on him. Poor fellow! But how fortunate that he could not see me; I was completely unnerved.

(*Enter Doctor and William, L. They move to the tent where the Captain was taken.*)

William. Dar doctor, he is in dar.

(*They enter the tent. William comes out immediately.*)

William. Yes, sah. I'll hab a bucket ob water dar in de twinklin' ob a lam's tail!

(*Exit L.*)

Milroy. I wish I knew how badly he is injured. But it won't do for me to go in there.

Sentry. Say, old pal, what's the row?

Milroy. An officer's horse has fallen and injured him.

Sentry. Oh! is that all? Say, old pal, you wouldn't mind giving me another pull at that glass friend of yours?

Milroy. Oh, no; you are welcome.

(*Milroy turns his back to the officers' quarters to give the drink to sentry They talk together. Connery looks from the tent. Re-enter William, L., with bucket.*)

William. Yere is de water! Yere it is, doctor!

7

(*William enters the tent and comes therefrom directly with the Captain's coat.*) Did any white man eber see such a looking coat as dis yere? (*Paper drops from the coat.*) What's dat? Mighty big paper dat. (*Takes it to the fire, stoops to read. Spells.*) C–l–a–r–e–n–c–e, Klarance! What's dis? K–i–n–g. King! Why, dis yere am about de massa King! P–a–r–d–o–n, Pardon! What!! Oh, golly, golly! But dis yere must go to massa King befo dis nigger sleeps.

(*William drops the coat. Exit L., hastily.*)

(*Connery leaves the tent and moves to the rear and left and conceals himself. Col. Mc. appears on the portico.*)

Colonel. Orderly! Here, orderly!

Milroy. Here, sir! (*Salutes.*)

Colonel. Orderly, take these papers to the adjutant's quarters. Ask him to please look them over to-night. Tell him they came by to-night's mail. You can then be excused for the night.

(*Milroy takes the papers. Colonel re-enters the house.*)

Milroy. (*Aside.*) What if the paper were here? (*Peers about and looks at the papers.*) I can't see here. (*Moves to the fire.*) That's not it, nor that. (*Starts.*) Merciful heavens! Here it is. (*Reads*) "Henry Eaton," he gave that name. "Hung!" "Approved." (*Pushes this paper into his pocket.*) But the others — I must deliver them, or I shall be suspected before I can get away.

(*He enters the office tent, leaves the others, and moves towards the fire. Connery watching.*)

Sentry. Say, old pal! Getting cold, ain't you? You have been dismissed, you have.

Milroy. Yes; I was a little cold, but I am going to camp now; good night!

Sentry. Good night, old pal! Turn out early in the morning, old pal!

(*Sentry paces back to Milroy.*)

Milroy. Oh, yes! (*Connery watching. Milroy moves to the fire.*) Let me be sure. Yes, yes! This is the paper. (*Looks about, and lights it. Connery approaches,*

and when it is about half burnt.) Safe ! Thank God !
Safe for the present !

(*Connery lays his hand on Milroy's shoulder from behind.*)
 Lieut. Connery. Yes, safe !

 (*Tableau. Scene closes, — flats in front.*)

ACT FOURTH.

SCENE FOURTH.

(*A wood, same as scene second, third act. Enter private
 Scot, R., apparently unarmed; his coat is open, but he
 carries a pistol under his coat.*)

Scot. Here it is six o'clock in the morning, and that
cove, Milroy, not yet in camp. Jumped his bounty so
quick. Here he gives me fifteen dollars (*takes out the
bills*) to play sick, and let him have my post at old Mac's
headquarters. But blow me, if I can make out what he
wanted there. He might have cut from camp, if he wanted
to shake us — he could. Oh, I guess he didn't know any
better, and hived in with some of those head-quarter rib-
roasters. Won't they skin him at draw? That Sergeant
is a natural carder he is. Fifteen dollars ! and I says, I'll
go down to the sutler's and jerk me a pair of them high
top boots — I will. (*Discovers a citizen approaching.*)
Hullo, that old Johnny has just bought a pair of them
boots. Them's my boots. (*Enter citizen, L.*) Hullo !
old secesh ! How's your family?

Citizen. Good morning, stranger ! My family is right
well, I reckon, considerin' how we are druv up. Stranger,
this war has ruined me ! I have lost ten likely niggers,
all my stock, last week your people tuk the old mar, and
now my daughter has run off with one of your officers.

Scot. Kind of rough, Johnny. Say, Johnny, what
time is it?

Citizen. (*Nervously.*) I don't know what time it is, — on my honor as a gentleman, I don't know, sir.

(*Soldier draws his pistol, moves quickly on the citizen, and presents it.*)

Scot. Say, Old Dominion, shell! I want that *ticker*, I do.

Citizen. 'Fore heaven, sir, I really don't know what time of day it is. 'Fore heaven, I don't, sir.

Scot. No chin! Shell! or I will start a new Southern graveyard!

(*Citizen gives Scot the watch.*)

Citizen. Stranger, that watch has been in my family twenty years.

Scot. Oh, cheese it! that's too long for a watch to be in any one family. I will keep it in mine a few days for a change. (*Points to his boots.*) Rebellion, come up out of them boots!

Citizen. Stranger, I have just bought these boots at your sutler's, down there. Stranger, my darter is to be married to-morrow to the officer, and I —

Scot. (*Interrupting.*) Come up! (*He pulls off the boots. Scot moves off and pulls off his boots.*) Issue me them mud hooks! (*They exchange boots.*) Say, Johnny, do you live inside the lines?

Citizen. No, stranger. I got a pass to come in and buy —

Scot. Come down with that pass?

Citizen. But, stranger, if I am found inside the lines without a pass, I shall be arrested as a spy.

Scot. That's my little game. Come down with that pass! (*Citizen gives Scot the pass.*) But I will see you out of the lines; I knows the fellers on picket. Fall in, chivalry! Squad about face! (*The citizen faces about as Scot aims the pistol at him.*) Forward, march! (*They move slowly to the left.*) Oh, I'll see you safely out of the lines. There is nothing mean about me. Oh, no! Only I'm poor — I am — and I have to provide for myself.

(*Exeunt, L. Scene closes. Flats in front.*)

ACT· FOURTH.

SCENE FIFTH.

(*Captain Fitzhugh's head-quarters same as before; 8 A.M. The captain is seen in his bed. Lieutenant Thompson near, smoking and reading. A drill call outside. Capt. F. sits up in bed. He has on his trousers and stockings and woollen shirt.*)

Capt. F. Mr. Thompson! Was not that the drill call?

Lieut. Thompson. Yes, sir; it's now eight o'clock.

Capt. F. I had no idea it was so late. (*Feels of his neck and side.*) Mr. Thompson; I'm as stiff as one of those wooden Indians in front of the tobacco stores! Blazes! But I feel as if I had been used for a foot ball.

Lieut. Thompson. Well, Captain; you were lucky to get off without any broken bones, considering that you run your horse directly into a ditch, some four feet deep, near head-quarters. When they brought you here I thought we should have to plant you, Captain.

Capt. F. Plant me! Run my horse into a ditch! Why didn't the horse know enough to keep out of the ditches? According to your view of the case, it came near being my " last ditch." Eh, Thompson? May I trouble you for my coat? There is a paper in it I wish to examine,

Lieut. Thompson. Certainly. Your overcoat?

Capt. F. No, my frock coat. It's there, is it not?

Lieut. Thompson. No, Captain. You wore only your overcoat when they brought you here.

(*F. starts, — leaves the bed.*)

Capt. F. My coat not here? Here! William! William! where are my boots? What's the matter with that boy? Fire! fire! I dislike to excite William's hopes so early in the morning, Mr. Thompson, but I don't see my boots, do you?

Lieut. Thompson. William has not been here s' about nine o'clock, last evening, sir.

7*

Capt. F. What! William not here? Mr. Thompson, this company is getting demoralized.

Lieut. Thompson. Uncle Peter says he was not in camp last night. I will find your boots, Captain.

(*Exit C. R.*)

Capt. F. My coat missing, — and the pardon with it. I suppose they pulled off the coat when they took me into the Adjutant's quarters, and put me back into the overcoat because it was easier to get on. I didn't come up very smiling after that round with the ditch. Here! Orderly! Orderly!

(*Enter Orderly, R.*)

Orderly. Here, sir. (*Salutes.*)

Capt. F. Orderly, go over to regimental head-quarters and see if they have my frock coat there. Bring it here. Lively! Orderly! (*Orderly starts.*) Don't drop any papers from it! Mind, now!

Orderly. Yes, sir.

(*Exit Orderly, R. Re-enter Thompson with the Captain's boots, which gives to the Captain.*)

Capt. F. Thank you. (*He pulls on one, and commences to pull on the other.*) Where is Mr. Connery?

Lieut. Thompson. Don't know, Captain.

(*Capt. Fitzhugh stops with the boot half-way on.*)

Capt. F. Don't know? See here, Mr. Thompson, will you have the kindness to offer me a drink, and if I refuse it, I shall then know I am asleep, as I now more than half suspect. Is he on picket duty?

Lieut. Thompson. No, sir. He turned out very early, this morning, and I overheard one of the men say he went towards army head-quarters.

(*Rap outside.*)

Capt. F. (*Crossly.*) Come in!

(*Enter L., 1st Sergt. Harding.*)

Sergt. H. (*Salutes.*) Morning report, sir. (*Gives the Captain the report.*) One man missing.

Capt. F. What?

Sergt. H. One man missing, — Milroy, a recruit, sir. On duty at regimental head-quarters, last night; out of camp all night; not on post this morning.

Capt. F. (*Quietly; for he must show no feeling in the presence of the Sergeant.*) All right, Sergeant; dismissed. (*Sergeant salutes. Exit L. Then, vigorously.*) How many recruits have we received in my absence?

Lieut. Thompson. Six, sir.

Capt. F. And one of those high-price patriots jumps his bounty, so soon?

Lieut. Thompson. So it seems, sir.

Capt. F. Mr. Thompson, this command is going to the devil. My coat is lost, William disappears, Mr. Connery goes off kiting all over the country, and the men commence to desert, — all in twelve hours. We ought to be mustered out, and made sutlers, or Freedmen's Bureau agents.

Lieut. Thompson. Captain, I know you are not in the habit of drinking before breakfast, but I think a cocktail will do you good this morning. I know of no other remedy for all this, which is a mystery to me.

Capt. F. Do you, though? Well, Mr. Thompson, now I come to notice it, your head is quite horizontal on the top there. I think I will wet my Federal clay. But, make it a mild, lady-like ration, if you please, sir. (*Rap outside.*) Come in! (*Enter Doctor — (Surgeon Walker,) R.*) Good morning, friend Quinine!

Doctor. Good morning, gentlemen.

Lieut. Thompson. How do you do, Doctor?

Capt. F. Uncle Peter! uncle Peter!

Uncle Peter. (*Outside.*) Yes, sah.

Capt. F. Lay another plate for breakfast.

Uncle Peter. (*Outside.*) Yes, sah.

(*Doctor moves to the Captain, and feels of his pulse*)

Doctor. A little fever. Quiet, and rest, though, is all you need.

(*The Captain arranges his toilet. Thompson is mixing drinks.*)

Capt. F. Quiet and rest! This is a nice spot for quiet and rest! Doctor, what did you do with my coat last night!

(*Doctor meditates.*)

Doctor. I think your boy, William, took it to clean.

Capt. F. My boy, William! Was that peregrinating African at head-quarters last night, when I located myself there?

Doctor. Certainly; he was the first to find you.

Capt. F. And now he turns up missing.

Lieut. Thompson. Doctor, shall I mix you a cocktail?

Capt. F. Of course; the Doctor knows the efficacy of " commissary " in driving off the chills.

Doctor. If you please.

(*Raps outside.*)

Capt. F. Come in. (*Enter Col. McManus.*) Colonel, how do you do?

Colonel. Nicely, thank you, Captain. Good morning, Doctor. Good morning, Mr. Thompson. Putting up some of the Doctor's prescription?

Lieut. Thompson. Yes, Colonel; have one?

Colonel. Don't care if I do.

Doctor. He needs it.

Capt. F. Uncle Peter!

Uncle Peter. (*Outside.*) Yes, sah.

Capt. F. Lay another plate for breakfast.

Uncle Peter. (*Outside.*) Yes, sah.

Capt. F. Colonel, have you seen Mr. Connery this morning?

Colonel. No, Captain; why do you ask me?

Capt. F. Oh! for no especial reason. About half of my camp and most of my wardrobe is missing; he among the rest.

Colonel. I think he will turn up at the right time. It's a way he has.

Capt. F. (*Aside.*) What does all this mean? There is some mystery here. (*Raps outside.*) Come in.

(*Enter Orderly with coat. L.*)

Orderly. Coat, sir. (*Salutes.*)

(*Hands the Captain his coat, who feels for the Pardon, at once.*)

Capt F. (*Aside.*) Not here! Where did you find it, Orderly?

Orderly. The camp-guard had it. Found it on the ground, this morning.

Capt. F. Go directly back, and search where it was found. There is a paper missing from the pocket.

Orderly. Yes, sir.

(*Salutes. Exit, L.*)

Capt. F. (*Aside.*) William had this coat, and left it on the ground all night; and now he is missing, and the pardon also. What does this mean? (*Loudly.*) Gentlemen, there is going to be a first-class row in this army!

Colonel. How's that?

Doctor. What? } (*Together.*)

Lieut. Thompson. Captain!

Capt. F. Excuse me. I think my nerves are just a trifle weak this morning. As the first-family men say, " Come, gentlemen, let's liquor! "

Lieut. Thompson. Here they are.

(*He indicates the cocktails which he has mixed.*)

Capt. F. It is of no use, Colonel; fire won't bring that boy this morning.

Col. Indeed! Where is he?

Capt. F. That is just what I have been trying to ascertain. (*They get their dippers or mugs in hand and arrange themselves for the tableau, — the Colonel in the middle, Doctor and Thompson on his right (the left), and the Capt. on his left (the right.)* Gentlemen, I am — (*They raise their dippers or mugs. Rap outside. Pettishly.*) We shall never get this drink. Come in!

(*Enter Mrs. Fitzhugh and Clara Connery.*)

(*Tableau.*)

Clara. Where's Dick? Where's Dick?

(*She rushes about for him.*)

Mrs. F. Husband!

Capt. F. My wife here?

(*They embrace.*)

Clara. Where is Dick? Here, I must embrace some one.

Col. Me!

Doctor. Me!

Lieut. Thompson. Me!

(*Clara withdraws.*)

Clara. Excuse me, gentlemen. Please consider your-selves all embraced. But, Captain, where is Dick? He is — (*hesitates*) — he is not hurt, Captain.

Capt. F. Oh, no! He was all right at daylight this morning, and as he has not been in action since with any-thing stronger than commissary, I think he is safe enough now. He will be here soon, I hope.

Clara. Oh, thank you, Captain, thank you.

Capt. F. Gentlemen, excuse me. In the excitement of this rather unexpected arrival of recruits, I have for-gotten to present you. Gentlemen, — Mrs. Fitzhugh, and Miss Clara Connery, my first officer's gushing sister.

Clara. Oh! Captain!

Capt. F. Ladies, — this is our Colonel, Colonel Mc-Manus; and this is our surgeon, Dr. Walker. He is not the original Dr. Walker, for you will notice he wears the regulation clothing above his boots. And this is my second officer, Mr. Thompson. Clara, you will remember Mr. Thompson as our first sergeant, when we left home.

Clara. (*To T.*) I am happy to meet you, Lieutenant.

Lieut. Thompson. Thank you.

(*They step aside together, and take a position on the right, tolerably near the right door. Mrs. Fitzhugh is on the right of her husband, the Captain; the left, the Doctor; and the Colonel on the right of the Doctor, — the left of the stage.*)

Capt. F. Uncle Peter!

Uncle Peter. (*Outside.*) Yes, sah.

Capt. F. Lay two more plates for breakfast.

Uncle Peter. (*Outside.*) Yes, sah.

Capt. F. Is not this a perfect surprise, Colonel?

Mrs. F. As we intended to make it.

Capt. F. As much, Captain, to *you*, as it was two hours since to *me*.

Capt. C. Yes; it is a perfect success. And if Mr. Connery were only here to see Clara.

(*Enter Connery with Bessie Moore in her proper costume,*
R. All start.)

Lieut. Connery. Yes, Connery is here. (*Discovers Clara.*) Clara, you here?

Clara. Dick! Oh, Dick!

(*They embrace.*)

Capt. C. Is it possible? Miss Bessie Moore here?

Lieut Connery. Yes, she seems to be now. But I was in doubt about it, yesterday.

Capt. F. Mr. Connery, please illuminate this subject.

Lieut. Connery. Yes; perhaps, though, the Colonel can do it better.

Capt. F. The Colonel? More and more mystery. Doctor, please experiment on me, and let me know who I am, and where I am.

(*All laugh.*)

Col. Yes, Captain. Briefly, this is your missing recruit, *private Milroy!*

Capt. F. Bessie Moore in Federal blue?

Bessie. Indeed I was, yesterday.

Col. Yes. Captain, Private Milroy enlisted in our regiment to save Henry Eaton, who is not Eaton, but Clarence King, and for whom Miss Moore has something of a liking. Private Milroy induced the Sergeant to detail him to our head-quarters last night, to enable him to destroy the findings of the court, and thereby gain time for his friends to secure a pardon.

Capt. F. Yes, Colonel, but he is already par —

Col. Excuse me, Captain; Private Milroy succeeded in destroying the papers, and Mr. Connery —

Lieut. Connery. Yes; Connery happened to detect the fair incendiary in the act, and took him, — her, — to the Colonel's quarters.

Bessie. And the Colonel's lady kindly loaned me this suit, which, perhaps, better becomes me than did the uniform.

Capt. F. This is wonderful! Do you know, Colonel, this reminds me of the Arabian Nights business. Excuse me; I have forgotten to present you, Be,— Miss Bessie. Well, perhaps you all feel pretty well acquainted; at least, you ought to by this time if you don't. But, Mr. Connery, why were you up so early this morning?

Col. To get the approval at army head-quarters of Private Milroy's discharge.

Lieut. Connery. Yes; here it is.

(Gives it to Bessie.)

Bessie. Thank you, Mr. Connery.

Capt. F. Oh yes! You have all done considerable in the sensation and surprise line; *now* for my turn, for our work is not yet completed. As to the pardon —

(Enter Clarence King and Wm. R.)

Wm. Wherefo' am de job not done? Massa Captain, yere is de pardon! *(Holds out the pardon which Connery takes.)* And yere is de man! *(Bessie and Clarence King rush into each others arms, and Wm. shuffles.)* Dat's right! Dat's right!

Capt. F. What's this? Why, this was to be my part of the sensation business; but never mind. *(Bessie and King separate.)* Be—, Miss Bessie, this, I suppose, is the happy man?

Bessie. Indeed, he is.

Clarence. Indeed, I am. And, Captain, I thank you. I—

(The Captain interrupts.)

Capt. F. Oh, never mind that, old fellow. I only did a man's duty.

Clarence. And, I thank you all, including my faithful and true friend here, William.

William. Yes, Massa King, dis am a big day for dis yere camp.

Bessie. Mr. Connery, *(Connery comes forward)* I wish to thank you, sir, for your manly consideration and great kindness. Now, *(she takes Clarence by the hand)* now, I think I can say, — safe, at last!

Lieut. Connery. (*Giving the pardon to King.*) Yes,— now — safe!

Capt. C. Uncle Peter! uncle Peter!

Uncle Peter. (*Outside.*) Yes, sah.

Capt. C. Uncle Peter, lay all the plates for breakfast.

Uncle Peter. (*Outside.*) Yes, sah.

(*Uncle Peter thrusts his head through the cook-room door.*)

Uncle Peter. (*Aside.*) What de debil is de matter yere?

Capt. F. My friends, — a short time since, and before my family got to be so happily extensive as it now is, we were about to take something for the chills. I think, *now,* we will postpone it, until I can send to the sutler's and procure something that will enable the ladies to join us, *when,* if you please, we will drink to this sentiment : —

" May the deplorable events which now distract our unfortunate country, terminate as happily as these adventures seem likely to end."

(*Tableau.*)

(*Curtain down.*)

8

www.ingramcontent.com/pod-product-compliance
Lightning Source LLC
Chambersburg PA
CBHW032349020726
47499CB00008B/2687